Loving Gigi

The Andrades

Ruth Cardello

Author Contact

website: RuthCardello.com

email: Minouri@aol.com

Facebook: Author Ruth Cardello

Twitter: RuthieCardello

Gigi Bassano

Young. Beautiful. Idealistic. Proud. Gigi was raised outside the Andrade clan, but it has left her with an ache she cannot deny. When she's invited to her brothers' weddings, she refuses at first, then changes her mind and attends without telling anyone. She won't let herself love them, but she can't stay away. It's a recipe for disappointment and heartbreak.

Especially when she throws herself at her brother's best friend, Kane.

Kane Sander

Sexy, rich, loyal, protective. He shouldn't want her. But he will.

He should stay away from her. But he won't.

Love doesn't follow anyone's rules. Deny it. Run from it. Love always finds a way.

Be the first to hear about my releases

ruthcardello.com/signup

One random newsletter subscriber will be chosen every month in 2015. The chosen subscriber will receive a $100 eGift Card! Sign up today by clicking on the link above!

Copyright

Print Edition

An original work of Ruth Cardello.

All Rights Reserved. No part of this book may be used or reproduced in any manner whatsoever without written permission from the author, except in the case of brief quotations embodied in critical articles and reviews.

This book is a work of fiction. The names, characters, places, and incidents are products of the writer's imagination. Any resemblance to actual persons, places, events, business establishments or locales is entirely coincidental.

Dedication

To all of my readers who came out to see me in London and Edinburgh. Thank you for the warm welcome. I truly enjoyed my time there and will treasure my memories from both.

Note to my readers

For now, Loving Gigi is the final book in the Andrade Series, but I have enjoyed being in this world so much that you'll see these characters again in my next series:

THE BARRINGTON BILLIONAIRES.

(Releasing this Fall.)

Chapter One

"Where's your uniform?" a sharply dressed blonde woman in a black pants suit with a stark white shirt barked.

Gigi Bassano froze in the doorway of the kitchen. She had hoped to slip through, unnoticed, but the impatient woman before her had spotted her instantly. Gigi cursed the simple, blue cotton slacks and plain white blouse she'd worn. *Just my luck. I look like staff.* She would have dressed more formally, but that would have required admitting to herself she wanted to attend the wedding.

From the moment she'd received the first invitation to this ridiculous, quadruple island shindig, she'd told herself she wasn't interested. She didn't belong there. She wasn't an Andrade; she was a Bassano. The bastard child of a man who had died eleven years earlier. Some children heard fairy tales of maidens meeting princes as bedtime stories; Gigi's father had read his young daughter newspaper articles highlighting the achievements of her brothers. He'd always said he would introduce her to them one day, and they would love her as he did.

Her father had died before keeping that promise. Many of her memories of him had faded as the years passed, but the pain of his departure remained.

Gigi could have forgiven him for having two families. She loved him enough to pardon that weakness. What had been inexcusable, however, had been the ache he'd cultivated inside her for a family who had turned out to be nothing like he had described them.

Gigi had only seen her brother Gio in person one time, but that was more than enough. He had come to collect their father's body from Venice. Gigi had overheard him speaking to her mother. He'd treated Leora as if she were nothing and had ended the conversation by threatening to take their home if her mother ever spoke of her relationship with Gio Sr.

Witnessing that exchange had shaken Gigi. Not only had her father left her, but he had lied to her as well. There was no family waiting to meet her. And the disgust Gigi had heard in her eldest half-brother's tone when he had spoken to her mother had filled her with shame. A deep, manifesting fear had taken root in the young woman she'd been.

Her mother was nothing but a rich man's mistress.

She was the irrelevant child, not even worth a mention.

It even rocked her pride in her Venetian heritage. Born Gigia, Gigi Anglicized her name. She didn't care that it made her sound more masculine. From that day on, she'd called herself Gigi and sought to distance herself from what she couldn't understand.

She told her mother she wanted to study in England and

made a good argument for the merits of a private boarding school. Back then she'd been innocent to the burden her request would place on her mother. She had no idea the expense her mother already had by trying to maintain the palazzo they lived in. Her young eyes hadn't noticed the furniture and the paintings slowly disappearing as her mother sold them off to finance Gigi's education.

Leora Bassano had worked two jobs for as long as Gigi could remember, but it wasn't until recently that Gigi had begun to understand why. Without complaint, her mother had sacrificed so Gigi could have more.

Part of Gigi wanted to crawl back onto her mother's lap and beg her to forgive her. *I've spent so many years as ashamed of her as I've been of myself. Am I wrong to judge her? I know my mother is a good woman. She loves me completely, unconditionally.*

Why can't I love the same way?

Part of her wanted to shake her mother for never demanding more from her father or from her daughter. Why hadn't Leora fought for the man she loved? Why had she accepted the choices a young and angry Gigi had made?

And why did she continue to keep their palazzo on the Grand Canal? Why not sell it or at least wipe all memory of him from it?

When asked, her mother always said she'd loved Gio, and she would always love the home he'd given her. Photos of Gio's American sons were still scattered throughout every room as if they were part of her own family. The sight of those photos sickened Gigi.

Her brothers didn't care for either of them any more than her father had.

Trying to explain that to her mother, though, was an act of futility. A few years ago, Gigi had threatened to stop visiting the palazzo until her mother disposed of the photos, but Leora had refused. She'd merely said, "This is your home, but it is mine as well. You are free to come and go. Home is not a cage; home is a place you leave when you must . . . and return to as often as your heart draws you back."

Which was her mother's way of saying, "Do whatever you want, and I will do the same."

"Do you speak English?" the woman before her asked, calling Gigi back to the present.

"Yes," Gigi answered automatically.

"And Italian?"

"Yes."

"Clara said she'd hired bilingual staff for today, but half of them clearly aren't. How can I be expected to have everyone where they need to be if they can't understand what I'm saying?" The woman spoke at breakneck speed that would have been difficult for Gigi to understand had she not gone to a private school in England. "You do understand me, don't you?"

"Perfectly."

"Thank God. You're the only one."

"Perhaps if you spoke more slowly?" Gigi suggested, while looking for a way to extricate herself from the conversation.

"I don't have time to repeat myself a hundred times. What position were you hired for? Server? Cleaning staff?"

Gigi started to answer, but stopped when the truth would have exposed her. "No, I—I . . ."

With an impatient wave of her hand, the woman said, "Whatever it was, you've been promoted. The next hour is the pre-ceremony reception. Drinks are supposed to be circulating. I don't know why I couldn't have used my all-English-speaking staff. Does anyone really need to be handed a drink by someone who speaks their native language? Champagne is a universal concept." She handed Gigi a paper and pointed toward a side kitchen door. "If you can get the cluster of servers who are bumbling around in the next room to pick up their trays and disperse into the crowd on the lawn, I will pay you double whatever you were promised."

Gigi considered telling the woman who she was, but knew it would stop her plan to covertly observe her brothers. "What's your name?" the woman asked brusquely.

"Luisella Romero," Gigi answered, giving the name of her childhood best friend.

"Nini Spark. Well, Luisella, don't just stand there. Come back here in an hour. By then I'll know if you earned your pay. Now get out there, and get those people circulating."

With a schedule in hand, Gigi exited the kitchen through a side door and entered a busy hallway. Just as Nini had said, the room was full of servers who were arguing in Italian because some had thought they'd been hired for different positions. None could understand a word Nini had said, but they were upset with her tone when speaking to them. Gigi considered dropping the list and walking past. This wasn't her problem.

Still, she felt badly for the staff, floundering without instruction. It would take so little to fix the situation before her. Her first attempt to gain the attention of the twenty or so people in the room went unnoticed, unheard over their loud commiserating. She raised her voice and spoke with authority in Italian. Without giving any of them time to question who she was, Gigi read off the list of where the servers were assigned. She fielded a couple questions that arose and made decisions based on what she thought would be best for all involved.

A sense of relief washed through the room, and they began to work with the bartender to fill their trays. In just a few short minutes the room was empty, and Gigi turned to head back into the hall.

"Impressive," a deep male voice said.

Gigi swung around to meet the appreciative eyes of a tall, broad-shouldered man whose tuxedo complemented his handsome looks. The conservative cut of his dark hair and the perfection of his tailored clothing were at odds with the notch on his nose that looked as if it had once been broken. He was polished, obviously wealthy, but tanned with strong hands like a man who made his living from manual labor.

He was gorgeous, but Gigi dismissed him after a quick once-over. Men like him were prowling for one thing, and one thing only. By twenty-two, Gigi had come across several like him—attractive men who thought women should drop to their knees before them in gratitude merely for being noticed.

Call me ungrateful, but I'm willing to wait for something real, not settle for what my mother had.

Without saying a word, Gigi moved to step past the man.

Instead of letting her pass, he stepped into her path and frowned. "Have we met before?"

You wish, Gigi thought, but remained silent. She raised her eyes to his, expecting to be left as disappointed as always, but became temporarily lost in his dark brown eyes. Her heart began to hammer in her chest. She told herself to look away but couldn't. Her breathing began to shallow as her body came alive beneath his sustained attention.

Subtle warmth began to spread through her, a need unlike anything she'd felt before. She'd had sex with a college boyfriend, but Nigel had never made her feel what this man did simply by looking at her.

So this is lust. Its intensity frightened Gigi. "No. Excuse me." She took a step forward, expecting him to step aside.

He continued to stand in her way. "My name is Kane Sander." His voice was a warm caress of its own. Gigi had a sudden desire to hear him say her name.

She opened her mouth to say it, when a sliver of sanity stopped her. No one could know she was there. Gigi's body hummed with a need she knew she would deny. Her mouth dried as she lied. "Luisella. Luisella Romero."

"Are you staff or family?" His question took her by surprise.

"Neither," Gigi answered huskily. "I was asked to help

out."

A slow, sexy smile spread across Kane's face as if she'd just promised to spend the night with him. "I'll look for you after dinner."

Gigi opened her mouth to tell him not to, but no words came out. He was no college boy. Kane was a man in his late twenties or early thirties, experienced and confident. His smile was as bold as sin, and full of just a dash of humor, as if he were inviting her to play along in some decadent game. On impulse, she asked, "What if I'm here with someone?"

Kane took her left hand in his and slowly, seductively, caressed the place where a ring might have been but was not. "I don't care who you came with, as long as you leave with me."

His touch was a fire that rushed through Gigi, scattering her thoughts until there was nothing except him and the yearning she felt for him. "Are you always so sure of yourself?" Her voice was as soft as a whisper.

"Only when I'm certain of what I want." He brought her hand up to his mouth, slowly kissing the spot he had caressed. "Before I met you I was wondering how I'd make it through what is promising to be a tediously long wedding. I'm still asking myself that, but now for an entirely different reason."

Wedding.

I'm here for a wedding. Not for this. She ripped her hand out of his, backing away as she did. "I have to go."

His smile widened. "Me, too." He inclined his head. "Until later."

Gigi turned on her heel and fled, disappearing into the crowd gathered in the foyer of the impressive and striking mansion. Despite the many people around her, she had never felt so alone.

I came even though I told my mother I wouldn't. I practically threw myself at a man who now thinks I'm going to spend the night with him.

What am I doing here?

✧ ✧ ✧

KANE WATCHED THE beautiful brunette rush off and took a moment to appreciate the perfection of her ass as she strode away. Luisella.

He didn't speak a word of Italian, but he had been instantly turned on by the sound of her issuing orders to the staff in the language. He groaned. She was likely in her mid-twenties and that normally wasn't his taste. His cock didn't care. It had sprung to attention at the first glance of her, the light scent of her, and most definitely at the sound of her.

He considered himself a discerning lover. At thirty-two, it wasn't about quantity anymore. He'd sown his wild oats, woken up beside a good share of women he'd enjoyed fucking, and now preferred short-term relationships over one-night stands. Since he'd taken over his father's company, he didn't have the time to look for new partners. Women came to him, and he welcomed their attention, but on his terms and only when it didn't interfere with work. Although his family was wealthier than most, he'd been raised to never take that for granted. His parents had made their fortune through hard work, and he would take the family company to the next level the very same way.

He chose women like himself. Successful. Realistic. Unlikely to shed a tear when he inevitably told them it was over. In general, he lived by the five-fucks rule. Less than five made dating too time consuming. Too much time spent getting to know someone new. More than five led to awkward expectations even though he was clear about his lack of desire for anything permanent.

Yes, five was the magic number.

Luisella looked young and, if the way she blushed at his proposition was anything to go by, relatively inexperienced. For a man like him, that spelled trouble with a capital T.

Still, he already couldn't stop thinking about her. She was beautiful, but he knew many beautiful women. He was a healthy male with a good appreciation for women and the variety of forms they came in. No, it was more than her delicate features or her tight little body. It was the punch of lust he'd felt at the sound of her voice. The way desire had licked through him just by standing next to her. Like a strong shot of Scotch, she'd gone straight to his head and muddled his thoughts. The brief touch of her skin against his mouth had just about done him in. He'd have to take the long way back to rejoining the wedding party, or they'd notice the still-throbbing evidence of how she made him feel.

A few minutes later, Stephan Andrade spotted Kane outside and walked over to join him. He was a tall blond man in an ocean of mostly dark-haired and olive-skinned relatives. "Gio is looking for you. Fifteen minutes until the ceremony starts. He and his brothers are gathering in the tent on the left side."

Kane frowned at the cousin of his best friend. It was difficult to put certain things aside. Even though it had been nearly two years since Gio had reconciled with his extended family, Kane knew too much about their history not to be cautious when it came to trusting any of them. Gio was like a brother, and he would defend him against anyone, even a blood relative.

He did his best to conceal his doubts, especially since his sister was marrying Gio's younger brother Nick and therefore would also be part of this family. *A quadruple wedding.* Kane had thought Rena was kidding when she'd told him Gio and his three brothers would all say their vows at the same ceremony. She claimed it was romantic. He'd thought she'd lost her mind at the time. However, as he saw the elaborate production the day had become, he had to admit it was nice to not have to attend three more weddings that year.

He shook his head as two children knocked into him before rounding the corner and disappearing. A frazzled woman was in hot pursuit. He and Stephan shared a look as she sped off after them.

"That's one nanny who won't last," Kane joked.

Stephan shrugged. "She's their mother. She's married to my second cousin from North Carolina. She says she wants two more."

Kane raised a skeptical eyebrow. "Is she sane?"

"You'd have to ask her husband," Stephan answered in a

light tone. "But you can never have too much family."

Kane looked around doubtfully. "In theory."

Stephan stood taller. "Do you have a problem with your sister marrying my cousin?"

Kane let out a long sigh. "A year ago I would have killed Nick for looking at Rena. Now I'd kill him if he left her. I've never seen her happier."

Stephan gave Kane an approving pat on the shoulder. "Good. Then come; everyone is waiting for you. Let's get this wedding going."

Kane walked with Stephan through the crowd that would soon move to sit in front of the blooming pergola in the field overlooking the ocean. Rena would describe this as beautifully interwoven vines of fall color—romantic. To Kane, it was greenery suspended from an overhead trellis. He scanned the area, recognizing and dismissing the rich and famous from all over the world.

When he finally located her, his little Italian beauty, he was surprised to see her standing off to one side of the group, with her arms wrapped across her as if she were self-conscious. He would have gone to her side if he hadn't been in the wedding party. He felt oddly protective of this woman he knew next to nothing about. That feeling gave way to something more, though, as soon as their eyes met. His breath caught in his throat. He hadn't imagined their attraction. It was there, just as strong, just as wild. He was a man used to being in control at all times, but as his cock stirred to life again, he felt deliciously willing to let her lead him wherever she wanted to go.

Luisella's eyes widened. She blushed as if she heard his thoughts and turned away.

"Do you know her?" he asked Stephan.

"Who?" Stephan turned, but he was too late. Luisella had slipped away around the side of the tent.

"Her name is Luisella Romero."

Stephan shook his head. "It doesn't sound familiar, but we have family and friends from all over the world here today. There are many people I don't know."

Me, too, Kane thought. *But there is only one I intend to get to know better.*

Much, much better.

Chapter Two

INSTEAD OF SITTING in the rows and rows of white chairs stretched out before the pergola, Gigi stood off to one side, half hidden behind a corner of a white tent. With what looked like five hundred people in attendance, and not all of them able to contain their children to seats, she was not the only one standing.

A hush fell over the guests as her four brothers took their places at one side of the pergola, standing from oldest to youngest. Gio, Luke, Nick, then Max. Each in a black tux with a different color flower boutonnière.

Three beautiful flower girls, ranging from what looked like two to six years of age, dance-walked down the aisle between the guests, dropping multi-colored rose petals as they went. Gio bent to say something to one of the flower girls. She smiled and hugged him before walking over to sit with her parents.

Pachelbel's Canon in D started and the guests all stood. A stunning bride in a simple, floor-length white dress walked slowly down the aisle, holding a bouquet of pink roses. Gio stepped forward to meet her as she approached the altar.

They stood facing each other and the bride's huge smile was heartwarming as was the tender expression on Gio's face.

Both confused Gigi. She hadn't expected Gio to have a softer side. She'd half-hoped coming to the wedding would allow her to confirm what she thought of him and his brothers. They were cold, awful people she was better off without in her life.

Her heart twisted in her chest when the scene before her implied the exact opposite. Luke took a step forward, his eyes shining with emotion as his bride walked down the aisle to meet him. She was visibly pregnant, but no less radiant. Her wedding dress was of a similar style, yet subtly different than the bride before. She took Luke's hand and moved to stand face to face with him, just off to the right of Gio and his bride. He touched her cheek softly, as if reassuring her.

Nick smiled widely as his bride walked toward him, and he jokingly checked his watch as if to imply she should hurry herself along. His bride shook her head in amusement and waved her bouquet at him in a playfully threatening manner. They took their place to the right, another strikingly attractive couple who looked head over heels in love with each other.

Max walked to his place on the end and held out his hand to his bride who stopped to wave at an older couple before joining him. She said something softly to Max that made him chuckle and glance back at his brothers before bending to give her a quick kiss.

Gigi had never felt more miserable in the face of such beauty. She wanted to run away, pretend she'd never come.

Yet she also wanted to step away from the tent and announce herself, somehow become a part of the day. The result was a sense of being trapped within herself, a feeling she was accustomed to.

The minister began to speak, but Gigi was lost in her own thoughts. She studied the people in the crowd. How many in the crowd were related to her? She recognized some from photos that still adorned her mother's house. Her father's two brothers were sitting with their wives less than a hundred feet from her. *Would they welcome me if they knew I was here? Or would I be a cause for embarrassment? The one they invited who was never supposed to come.*

She wanted to wave to them, gain their attention somehow, but she didn't. Even after she'd moved to England, she'd dreamed they would seek her out. She'd kept a part of her heart open to them only to face more than a decade of indifference from them. *I could have handled threats from you. But to never even acknowledge me was the ultimate rejection.* No, she would never give them a chance to do that again.

So why am I here?

A female voice startled her. "Are you okay?"

Gigi sniffed and blinked away tears she didn't realize had been close to the surface. She turned and met the steel green eyes of a tall, beautiful red-haired woman with an American accent. "Yes, thank you."

"Do you need anything? A drink perhaps?" the woman asked smoothly, assessing her state as she spoke.

Gigi felt exposed before her, as if this woman saw straight through her. She shot the woman a vague smile and turned away, "Thank you for asking, but I'm fine."

"You're not alone, Gigi. If you need anything this weekend, call this number."

Gigi's head snapped around, but she didn't reach for the card the redhead held out. She took a deep breath and said, "You must have me confused with someone else."

One beautifully sculpted ginger eyebrow arched. "I don't make those kind of mistakes. Take the card."

Gigi took the card and held it out to read. It was black with a phone number written in white print. She turned it over. No other information. She placed it in the front pocket of her cotton slacks. "If you're hoping I'll pay for your silence, I can barely afford my plane ticket home."

The redhead held her eyes steadily. "Your secret is safe with me."

"Really? Why?"

The woman turned back to watch the wedding ceremony as she answered. "Because I know what it's like to be on the outside looking in. It's not easy."

"Who are you?" Gigi demanded. She didn't like feeling this woman knew all about her while she knew nothing about the woman.

"A friend if you need one," the woman answered softly.

Gigi turned to the ceremony in frustration, then back to where the woman had been standing, but she was gone. She glanced around but didn't see the redhead anywhere. "Well, that was creepy," she muttered to herself.

When she turned back to the wedding ceremony her breath caught in her throat. Kane was standing at the top of the aisle reading a poem about love and family. He caught her watching him and smiled before continuing. Gigi fought against the pleasure that seared through her from that simple connection.

A deep sadness followed. *What do I know about either love or family? No one has ever loved me that way. I doubt they ever will. Sappy wedding poems don't reflect the reality most people live.*

Her emotions were already all over the place; did her libido need to add to the chaos?

Oh, God, weddings are dangerous. They make you want to believe love can be beautiful, that it can last. Four couples were swearing before God and family to remain faithful. How many would keep that vow? Their father hadn't, and Gigi was evidence of how little respect her mother had for the institution.

Kane's deep voice listed the attributes of true love and the importance of tending to it, and a sudden jaded thought came to Gigi. *He's probably married.*

His wife is probably sitting in one of those rows thinking he's talking about their marriage, while he's looking at me. He paused as if he'd become as wrapped up in her as she was in him. Gigi felt better and worse all at the same time. Her brain was listing all the reasons why she should look away, but beneath his hungry gaze her body screamed, "Hell, yes!"

Of course I want him. Look at him. He's perfect. Ruggedly sexy, but hotter than hell in a tux. *All this proves is that I'm human. I'm sure half the women here are looking at him and imagining a romp with him.* He winked at her and her lips parted with a wistful sigh. Gigi fought a crazy desire to walk straight up to him and test if his lips would feel as good on hers as they had grazing her hand.

"There you are," Nini said from beside her in a brusque American manner. "I told you to come back and see me in an hour. I don't like looking for people."

Great. Gigi was tempted to admit she didn't work for her, but trying to explain her way out after what would follow would be worse than playing along one more time. The less attention she brought to herself the better. "Sorry, I got distracted." She referenced the wedding ceremony. "It's different than I expected."

A flash of something akin to understanding passed over Nini's expression, then her eyes were hard and determined again, and she spoke in a fast, impatient tone. "It's like watching a fairy tale, isn't it?"

"Yes," Gigi said softly as she looked around at all the children who were woven in and out of the ceremony. Today, the Andrades were the family her father had described. Old memories swept through her, making her yearn to speak to her father one last time. She had so many questions.

Papa, did you love us as much as you loved them?
Was I ever more than your secret shame?

Nini cut into her thoughts with a dose of reality. "It's okay to look, but don't want it. It's not real. Not for people like us. You and I are nothing beyond what we do for them. We're only as valuable as how seamlessly we deliver our services. Make a mistake and we're discarded like a chair with a broken leg."

Ouch. Gigi looked at the glittering blue eyes of the woman beside her and wondered what had happened that had made her so bitter. She spontaneously asked what she was wondering. "If you don't like your job, why do you do it?"

Nini frowned at her and said harshly, "I love what I do, but you remind me of myself when I was your age. All starry-eyed. People like that get used and discarded. You're here to do a job and then leave. Don't think just because you're standing on the same grass as they are that you could ever be one of them." Nini cleared her throat. "You did well with the pre-ceremony cocktails. Do you think you could get our international crew to serve dinner just as smoothly?"

Why not? Gigi asked herself in resignation. She was a hot mess on the inside. Helping out might help her clear her head. She nodded and followed Nini back to the house where the food was being prepped. On autopilot, she translated Nini's instructions to the staff and then slipped back to the wedding just in time to watch the guests begin to fill the large tent that had been set up over a dance floor and a sea of tables.

Afterward, she stood near the back entrance of the dinner tent and sighed sadly. *I could be at one of those tables if I'd answered the invitation. I could say something now, and maybe they would welcome me in.*

Maybe.

Nini's right, though. Just because I'm standing here beside them, doesn't make me one of them. Why are they contacting me now? What do they want from me?

Could they possibly want to know me as much as I've always wanted to know them?

And what if they don't? I'm happy with my life. I don't need to rip open old wounds.

One of her uncles walked by and their eyes met briefly. She sent him a tentative smile, and he nodded in her direction. Cordial, but not warm. He showed no sign of recognizing her as he continued to walk past her.

Her heart tightened painfully in her chest.

He doesn't know me. Why should he?

I'm not one of them.

Not when I was little. Not now.

Gigi turned and fled the area. She tried to leave the party, but there was no easy way out, and she didn't want to see Nini again. She headed toward the stairs of a steep bluff that led to the beach. She only made it halfway down the steps before she stopped, leaned on the railing of the landing, and cried softly into the ocean breeze.

I shouldn't have come.

This was a bad, bad idea.

Feelings she'd bottled up came spilling out. She cried out in anger then broke down into tears. Memories she'd pushed aside for so long came back with agonizing vividness. She was back at the palazzo in Venice, running into her father's office to see him after school. As if watching a movie, she saw herself calling to him softly, thinking he was asleep in his leather chair. Then shaking him with growing fear as he didn't respond.

Her young mind had fought against the truth even when it was obvious. In shock, she'd sunk to her knees at his feet and wept into his still-warm hands. He had left her. Just like that. No goodbyes. No warning.

When her mother had pulled her from him, Gigi had fought her, transferring some of her anger to her mother. *I hated him for leaving, and I hated my mother for not being angry with me.*

As her tears dried, Gigi continued to look out over the water. She had never felt more alone or more confused. Now that she'd graduated from college she was free to go anywhere, but even that freedom was suddenly terrifying. *I have nothing and no one.*

Real loneliness swept up and through her. There was an emptiness within her she desperately wanted to fill with something. Anything. Had she been a drinker, she would have snuck back into the wedding and numbed herself with alcohol. Instead, she watched the sunset and made a frivolous wish.

For just one night, could I actually be the woman Kane thinks I am?

Someone who isn't afraid to take what she wants.

✧ ✧ ✧

THE CEREMONY WAS beautiful but long. Kane kept a smile plastered to his face during the photo session that followed. It wasn't that he didn't appreciate the importance of the event or wish each couple well. His sister, Rena, had found a man she said she couldn't live without. Just because it wasn't who he would have chosen for her, didn't mean it couldn't work. And, he had to admit, Nick had grown into a solid businessman. He was glad he hadn't done as he'd threatened and strangled him when he'd first heard they were dating.

Watching Gio walk off with Julia had left Kane feeling conflicted. On one hand, Gio had found happiness with a woman who had helped him reunite with his family. Two years ago, Gio wouldn't have been able to stand being in the same room with his brothers for longer than five minutes, never mind sharing an altar with them. Now they were the family they'd always been meant to be. Although Kane was happy for them, he couldn't help but feel that an era was ending. His sister wouldn't need him to protect her anymore. Gio would no longer spend holidays with the Sanders. They each had their own families now and this island to gather on.

Kane imagined himself with a wife and kids and shuddered.

Not yet.

There isn't a woman on the planet I'd give up my freedom for. Although, I may have found one I'd break my rule of five for. A woman like Luisella would be worth the mess that dating longer inevitably brings.

He searched the dining area for her and was disappointed when he didn't see her. Alessandro Andrade was welcoming everyone, but Kane was already plotting his escape. He had planned his speech, but shortened it as he became more and more impatient. He scanned the room again and met the eyes of several beautiful women. Some looked away and blushed. Some met his gaze boldly. All of them left him cold.

At Gio's urging, Kane accepted a microphone and delivered the speech Rena had helped him write. She hadn't trusted him to sound sentimental enough, and her instincts were spot on as usual. He briefly described Gio before he'd met Julia as a gruff workaholic. He smiled at Julia when he described how she'd come into his friend's life and turned it upside down. Sometimes even a successful man can benefit from a smack in the head. He toasted the couple and their future together.

When he finished, Gio stood and gave Kane a brotherly hug. His new wife, Julia, hugged him tearfully. As soon as the microphone was handed off to a man Nick knew, Kane made his way to the side of the tent and slipped outside.

The sun was setting on the horizon and the area that had been full of chairs was already cleared. When Kane saw what looked like a small carnival being set up, he shook his head in amusement. The Andrades were an eccentric family. They had more dignitaries, royals, and CEOs of companies attending than many political summits, but they filled the lawn with entertainment for their children. He could see what his sister loved about them and had no trouble imagining her chasing her own children around these island mega mansions.

Still. Bounce houses, cupcakes, balloons? He shuddered at the scene he knew would unfold there as soon as the mass of children, who were sitting beside their parents beneath the tent, were released into the wild. Kane walked closer to the bluffs, looked out over the ocean and savored what was likely the last quiet to be found. It was then he caught a slight movement on the steps leading down to the water and instantly straightened.

It had to be. He called out softly, "Luisella."

The woman didn't turn at first. She stayed where she was, midway down, staring out over the crashing waves. Her hair that had been tied back in a sophisticated knot flew wildly in the air behind her. As if she suddenly became aware of someone watching her, she turned and looked up at him.

Oh, yes.

The night air sizzled with what could only be described as their animalistic attraction to each other. He wanted her, and he would have her.

Hopefully that night, repeatedly, and then again in the morning. He started down the steps, forcing himself to take them one at a time. He didn't want to rush through one moment of what he knew would be an unforgettable night.

As he neared her, he noticed the emotional shine to her eyes and his gut twisted as his protective nature kicked in. He stood beside her on the landing. "So this is where you've been hiding."

She looked at him angrily. "Please go away."

Kane's head snapped back. Women didn't speak to him that way. Well, only his sister and only when she was upset. "Did something happen? Are you all right?"

"Shouldn't you be with your wife?"

Was that it? Did she think he was married and prowling? "I'm not married."

She turned her attention back to the waves before them

and shrugged. "It really doesn't matter either way."

Regardless of how many times he'd imagined a better ending to the night, he would have walked away as she asked, had he not noticed she was gripping the wooden railing so hard her knuckles were white. He put his hands on the railing beside hers and ignored how his blood rushed dizzily through him when their arms brushed slightly. "Are you here with someone?"

She kept her face averted. "Didn't you already say you didn't care if I was?"

Unable to stop himself, he put a hand beneath her chin and turned her face toward his. Even in the waning light he could tell she had been crying. "You shouldn't be alone right now."

One of her hands fisted on the railing, but she didn't pull her face away from him. Instead she said, "It doesn't matter what should or shouldn't be. Things are the way they are. Wishing for different only makes it hurt more."

Her accent was delightfully English. He rubbed a thumb across her jaw lightly, fighting how much he wanted to sample her pursed lips. "What happened, Luisella? Tell me." Fresh tears filled her eyes and Kane wanted to gather her to his chest and promise to fix it—whatever it was. Oh, yes, she was trouble, but nothing could have torn him from her side.

She looked into his eyes for a long time, and the fire he'd seen in them earlier returned. "Do you want to go somewhere? Leave here together?"

It was the last thing he expected her to say, and for a moment it left him speechless. Although her question had sent his blood rushing downward, he knew he wouldn't act on how she made him feel, not that night. She looked younger than she had earlier and lost in a way that made him want to save her more than he wanted to fuck her.

A battle raged within him when she slid her hands up his chest, wrapped them around his neck and pulled him down for a kiss. He knew he shouldn't, but he claimed her mouth gently, assured himself he could control the desire that seared through him at her touch. Her scent. The sweetness of her mouth as it opened to his. He deepened the kiss, almost against his will, and momentarily lost himself to the wildness of their attraction.

Her kiss tasted of angry abandon, and it brought him slowly back to his senses. She was hurting over something, and that wasn't how he wanted her to come to him. He pulled his mouth from hers. Their ragged breathing was as loud as the breaking surf below them. Very softly he said, "Slow down."

She went onto her tiptoes and kissed the side of his jaw. "I don't want to. I want to forget everything. Help me forget."

The innocence in her plea made Kane groan. "How old are you, Luisella?"

"Twenty-three," she said, arching against him desperately, trying to pull his head back down for another kiss.

"How old?" He hated that he didn't believe her.

"Twenty-two," she admitted. "But I'll be twenty-three soon."

Shit. He removed her arms from around his neck, holding her there before him like an errant child. "What happened at the wedding? Did you break up with your boyfriend?"

Once again sounding young and belligerent, Luisella answered defensively, "No, I didn't break up with anyone. What's wrong with you? I thought this was what you wanted."

I did. I do, he thought, *but not like this.* He stepped back from her. "You'll thank me one day. You're a beautiful young woman. Whatever is upsetting you tonight, sleeping with a complete stranger won't make it better."

Her face flushed beet red. "Are you lecturing me? Seriously? Fuck you." She turned to walk away.

On impulse he grabbed her arm and turned her around to him. His cock hardened at the exchange, and he told himself to let her leave, but he couldn't. Not yet. She pulled at her arm, but he didn't release it. Her glare only turned him on more. Still, he needed her to understand that she deserved better. "Many men would have taken you up on your offer, but they wouldn't have respected you the next day."

"But not you? Because what? You're a fucking saint?"

He laughed sardonically. "Hardly, and if you're going to keep swearing at me, at least vary your vulgarity."

"Fu—" Gigi started to say, then stopped. "I don't care what you think of me." She waved a finger angrily in his face. "You know why? Because when you're in hell it doesn't matter if someone turns up the heat. So laugh at me all you want, but you can't ruin what was already one of the worst days of my life."

She pushed past him, and Kane let her go. He had no right to stop her. She was upset, but she was better off without him. Being around her aroused him more than he expected, and he was close to making a huge mistake, if his throbbing cock was anything to go by. *Fuck, I shouldn't want her this badly.* He leaned over the banister and groaned. *She's probably here with her family.*

Shit, twenty-two. That's younger than my sister.

I almost slept with someone who might still have a curfew.

Chapter Three

STUPID. STUPID. STUPID.

As if coming to the wedding hadn't been a bad enough idea, she'd rounded off the day by completely humiliating herself. Gigi berated herself all the way up the steps, across the lawn, between the mansions, and down the long driveway. She was headed back to the tiny hotel room she'd been told she was lucky had still been available. She'd collect her things and leave on the next plane or boat out. She didn't care where to, as long as it was far from there.

The streets were dark and unlit. Although she'd walked to the wedding, navigating the streets was proving more difficult than she'd imagined. Still, that didn't stop her. She considered what she was walking away from to be far worse than whatever she might run into.

She stopped and covered her face with her hands. She'd heard Kane's laughter again and it tore through her. *I'm not a joke.*

I threw myself at a man, and he laughed.

Oh, my God. This is a new low, even for me.

I thought coming here would somehow make things better,

but it's worse. So much worse. She started walking again and stubbed her toe on a rock, almost falling onto the road, but righting herself at the last minute. It was then she realized she had no idea which road led back to her hotel. *What else could go wrong?*

A car pulled up beside her, and a male voice called out, "Do you need a ride?"

Gigi stepped back and put her arms protectively around herself. "No, just point me in the direction of the New Harbor Hotel."

The car pulled off to the side, and the driver hopped out. A tall light-haired man dressed in jeans and a T-shirt hustled to the passenger door. He held the door to the car open. "I would not be the best cabbie on Slater Island if I left you walking in the dark. Hop in, I'll drive you there."

"Thank you, but I'm fine."

The man, who looked to be about her age, held out his hand in greeting and the smile he flashed was harmlessly charming. "I'm Waffle."

"Waffle? Like the food?" She shook his hand and relaxed. It was difficult to be afraid of anyone with a nickname like that.

"Exactly," he said in a pleased drawl. "Who doesn't love them? I personally have never had one that wasn't delicious. How about you?"

Gigi shook her head, feeling the conversation was a bit unreal. "I never thought too much about it."

Waffle nodded slowly. "Many people don't. It's an underappreciated food item." He waved at the open door of the cab behind him. "So, do you want a ride?"

"Yes, I guess," Gigi conceded and slid into the back seat. Once they were driving again, she asked, "Did I miss the last boat off the island?"

"You sure did."

"How about the planes? Will they take me back to the mainland?"

"You won't find anyone free right now. Everyone's booked shuttling wedding guests back and forth."

"So I'm trapped here until tomorrow. Great."

Waffle looked in his rearview mirror at her then pulled into a driveway. Gigi tensed. *Oh, hell no.*

"What are you doing?" she asked in what she hoped was a voice that sounded more angry than scared.

"Give me two seconds. I'll be right back."

With duct tape? A shovel to bury me? Gigi watched the young man disappear into a house, and she jumped out of the car. She strode out of the driveway and was about to sprint down the road when she heard him calling for her.

"Hey, lady. Where are you going? I have something for you."

Gigi stopped and braced herself. She should have walked faster. She might have to stand and fight. "Really?" she asked sarcastically as she turned.

Waffle trotted up to her with a slice of pie on a plate and a fork. "My mom makes the best blueberry pie, and she swears it makes everything better." He held it out to her.

Gigi didn't raise a hand to take it.

A woman's voice called out from the house. "Waffle, are

you still out there? Does she want a drink to go with it? I have milk and water."

Waffle glanced back. "Hang on, Mom. I think I freaked her out by stopping here."

A woman in a bathrobe appeared in the driveway. She had a bottle of water in her hand. She waved Gigi and her son back to the driveway. She looked Gigi over with a critical eye. "You here for the Andrade wedding?"

Gigi nodded.

"You don't look too happy. Did you get fired or something?"

Gigi shrugged. "Or something."

"You in some kind of trouble?"

"No," Gigi said softly. She didn't know these people, but she got the sense they would have helped her had she said she was. "I just wish I hadn't come."

The woman took the pie from her son and handed it Gigi. "There's a reason why everything happens the way it does, even if we can't see it at the time. Have some pie."

Gigi accepted the offering with a sad chuckle. *Could the night get any stranger?* More out of politeness than anything else, she took a bite. It was delicious. Not quite good enough to erase years of yearning for a family who had ignored her or to make her feel less foolish about how she'd thrown herself at Kane, but it took the edge off both. She devoured the slice, took a few sips of the water the mother had brought for her, and got back into the cab with a slight smile on her face.

"Thank you," she called out as they pulled away.

Waffle's mother waved from the driveway. When they

were back on the road, Waffle said, "I was right, wasn't I? Don't you feel better?"

Gigi stared out the cab window into the darkness. "A little."

They pulled up in front of her hotel, and Waffle held the door open for her. Gigi dug through her pockets for money, but Waffle refused when she finally produced it. "Piece of advice?"

Gigi shrugged in resignation. "Sure."

"Whenever I feel really bad about something, I ask myself what I did to feel that way, and then I just don't do it again."

Gigi rolled her eyes. "Wisdom by Waffle."

He smiled, not bothered by her lack of faith. "Hey, I'm not the one who needed pie tonight."

There was no arguing that point, so Gigi didn't. She thanked him again and went into the small island hotel, grateful the day was finally over.

✧ ✧ ✧

KANE RETURNED TO the dinner tent a short time later and wasn't happy when he didn't see Luisella there. He cursed himself for not insisting he walk her back to . . . her family? . . . her disgruntled lover? Neither had held much appeal for him, but he should have put that aside to make sure she was safe.

His sister and her new husband were in the process of going from table to table to greet guests. Rena dragged Nick over as soon as she spotted Kane. "Where did you disappear to? Mom and Dad were looking for you."

Kane shot her a reassuring smile. "I was warm. I stepped outside to get some air."

Rena studied Kane's face, leaned in, and ordered softly. "Tell me you're happy for me."

Kane glanced over her shoulder at Nick then down again at his sister's concerned expression. "Of course I am."

Nick put an arm around Rena's waist and tucked her to his side. "We're family now."

Kane raised his eyes from Rena's and met his brother-in-law's eyes. "We always have been. I admit I didn't think you were good enough for her, Nick, but I would have felt the same about any man, I suppose. You make her happier than I've ever seen her, and that's all that matters to me. Take care of my little sister, Nick."

Nick chuckled and chided. "Or you'll wring my neck?"

"In a heartbeat."

"Good talk," Nick joked.

Rena rolled her eyes. "Kane, I'm perfectly capable of taking him out myself if I need to."

This time Kane laughed. "She is. You do not want to be on her bad side."

Nick nuzzled Rena's neck. "My little princess?"

Rena laughed and push his head away. "On their wedding day, my mother told my father he could leave her any time he wanted, as long as it was in a casket."

Nick threw back his head and laughed heartily. "It's true what they say. It's always the quiet ones. Your family looks nicer than mine, but I'll have to remember to watch my back."

"Be good to her, and you won't end up in the garden with her earlier boyfriends," Kane said with a straight face.

Rena burst out laughing when both of Nick's eyebrows rose dramatically. "He's kidding, Nick."

Kane held Nick's eyes, sending what he hoped was a clear message. There were no bodies in his family's garden—yet.

Nick nodded once subtly. Good, he understood. To lighten the mood, Kane brought two fingers to his eyes then motioned with them toward Nick and mouthed, "I'm watching you."

Rena laughed again, and Nick joined her.

Kane took a moment to scan the room again before asking, "Do either of you know a Luisella Romero?"

"I don't," Rena replied. "Why?"

Nick's smile widened. "I don't either, but it's interesting you're asking about her."

Kane made a growl deep in his throat before answering. "She looked upset earlier, and I want to make sure she's okay."

Instantly concerned, Rena looked around. "Oh, that's a shame. What does she look like? How old is she?"

"She's petite, long brown hair, beautiful dark eyes and she's—" Kane cleared his throat, "in her early twenties."

"Good for you." Nick whistled, then made a comical face and raised his hands in mock surrender when Kane frowned at him. "I don't judge."

"There is nothing to judge. As I said, she looked upset."

Nick looked down at Rena with a boyish smile. "He must have seen all that in her beautiful dark eyes."

Rena swatted at Nick. "Stop." She studied Kane's face again. "Luisella, huh? I'll ask around about her, but really? Early twenties?"

Kane made another sound of disgust. "I'm not interested in her."

Nick chuckled. Rena noticed Kane's temper rising and linked her arm with her husband's. "We didn't say hi to the Waltons yet. Let's head over there. I'll talk to you later, Kane."

"I hope you find her. I mean . . . I hope she's okay." Nick winked at Kane then turned to saunter off with Rena.

Kane circulated through the dining tent. He tried to forget about Luisella, but he couldn't. He found himself asking about her again and again, but no one knew her. No one had even heard of her.

Someone must have. She had to have come with someone, but with a wedding of that size, it wasn't as if Kane could ask every guest.

That would be crazy.

Especially for a man who had no intention of seeing her again.

Chapter Four

THREE YEARS LATER, Gigi sat on a bench in West Princes Street Garden in Edinburgh, Scotland, and unwrapped her meat pie, closing her eyes for a moment to enjoy the warmth of the spring day. The peace of the moment was broken by a familiar female voice.

"I thought you were going to the gym," Annelise Douglas said as she jogged in place beside the bench.

"I'm working out my arms today," Gigi answered as she brought her sandwich up to her mouth and defiantly took a bite.

Annelise kept jogging. "I hate that you can wallow in food and never put on weight." Just over five feet, Annelise was constantly battling her weight. She maintained her slender figure by living on salads and working out each day.

Gigi finished chewing then rewrapped the remaining portion. "I'd love to tell you I'm not wallowing, but it's my mother's birthday this weekend so I have to fly home tomorrow."

Stopping only to stretch one of her spandex-covered legs on the edge of the bench, Annelise said, "You love seeing your mother; what's the difference if she comes here or you go there?"

Gigi closed her eyes and sighed. "A big difference. Too many memories."

"Does she really live in a castle on the Grand Canal? What is that like?"

"It's a palazzo. More like a house that someone with a title once owned." Gigi raised her eyes to Edinburgh Castle, a beautiful backdrop to the city that had been her home since she'd graduated from college. "Nothing like a castle."

"Well, if my parents lived in Venice, I'd visit them all the time, palazzo or no palazzo. You can take me home with you any time."

No, I can't, Gigi thought. Annelise knew her well, but there were things Gigi preferred to deny even to herself. How confused visiting Venice made her feel was one of them. "Have you heard from Miss Fletcher?"

"She called this morning. She wanted to know if you had finished cataloging her aunt's estate."

"Finished last night. I emailed the auction house the list this morning. I thought I had sent it to her, too. I'll double-check. Tell her she should have a date by next week."

"Will do," Annelise said, stretching her arms above her head. "You'll be back on Monday, right?"

"Oh, yes," Gigi said. She didn't intend to stay in Venice one moment longer than necessary. She was happy in Edinburgh. Well, if not happy, at least content. She and Annelise had opened a small business. They connected people who had either high-end items or entire estates to sell off with people who could bring them the best price. It was commission work, but lucrative enough to allow Gigi to send money each month to her mother.

The perfect team. Annelise was a bouncy bookkeeping genius, and Gigi was the calmer face of their company with a good eye for antiques. Although they were young, they had built a reputation for impressive results that meant they didn't have to advertise. Clients found them.

Wiping her face with one of Gigi's napkins, Annelise plopped down beside her on the bench. "So, you're not interested in Greg?"

"Greg?"

"You know, the one who keeps dropping by with items to sell, one at a time, as if it's not obvious he's there to see you."

"Oh, Greg," Gigi said with new emphasis on his name. She sighed. "He's nice."

"I can't figure you out. You attract good-looking, seemingly normal men with money. They show up here like you ordered them from a catalog. I'd kill for some of the ones I've seen moon over you, but you sit home every Friday without a date. What are you waiting for?"

Gigi shrugged. "Money doesn't matter. I'm waiting for someone who makes me feel . . . a zing."

"A zing?" Annelise asked, amused by Gigi's word choice.

Gigi blushed. "You know what I mean. Your heart goes nuts. Your whole body feels like it's on fire. You want the person so much you can barely breathe."

"That's what you're waiting for?"

Gigi nodded slowly. "Yes."

Annelise stood and began to stretch again. "You need to stop watching those sappy old movies. That shit's not real."

Gigi looked up to the castle on the hill before her. In her mind, she was back on the bluffs of Slater Island again with Kane Sander. "I found it once."

Eyes round, Annelise asked, "Wait, are you referring to that guy you met right after college? At the wedding I'm sworn to never speak of?"

Gigi stood and gathered up her bag. "Yes. Forget I mentioned him. I don't like to remember that day." She still cringed every time she thought about how she'd behaved on that trip. Even though it had only been a few years, she felt a millennium older than the young woman who had been so afraid to get hurt that she'd snuck into her own brothers' weddings. When the humiliation of being turned down by Kane subsided, she had to admit he'd been right to walk away from her.

She would have regretted it, even if it had been good. She remembered their kiss on the bluffs, and warmth filled her cheeks. *It would have been great.*

Shaking her head, Annelise started jogging in place. "You know why it didn't work out with him? Because you were a hot mess that day. You had mope goggles on. They're worse than beer goggles. Anyone would have looked good to you. Forget that guy. You don't want to wake up at thirty and realize you missed out on some really great men because of this zing thing you imagined. You need to learn to move on. Same thing with Venice. Memories only have the power you give them. Go home and make your mother's birthday a special one. When you come back, ask Greg out. You might discover you like him."

"You are amazing, do you know that?" Gigi smiled and started walking beside Annelise.

Annelise smiled back. "Oh, I know." She gave Gigi a once over and said, "Now get your high-heeled, sophisticated arse back to the office. I'm going to run by the gym and take a quick shower. I'll call Miss Fletcher when I get back." She paused and added, "And don't you dare bring any cake to the office. I don't care how bad you feel."

Gigi was still smiling even after Annelise had run up the steps of the park and disappeared out the gate. The world according to Annelise.

A sudden, amusing thought came to Gigi.

Annelise was as wound up emotionally as Gigi was; she just talked a better game. She tended to date uptight men, and that didn't help her. *I wonder what she'd think of a man named Waffle?*

And pie?

✧ ✧ ✧

KANE RECOGNIZED THE high-pitched voice of Scarlet King before she entered the dining room of the posh, uptown restaurant. She was riding high on the success of her latest big screen release, but her voice carried as if she were still on Broadway. Although she was physically stunning, Kane found speaking to her a lot like watching a Saturday morning infomercial; he'd only do it if there were no other option.

His mistake had been fucking her the second time. He'd been drinking the first time, and she'd flirted with him outrageously at a dinner party they'd both attended. He'd been flattered, and she'd been willing. He couldn't say it was the best sex he'd ever had, but he was getting used to not being wowed. A week later they were at another mutual event, and she'd hung on him most of the night then followed him back to his limo. He'd been clear that if she came home with him, she wasn't staying over; he was too busy to be in a relationship with anyone.

It hadn't deterred her, and the sex had been marginally better but, a bit like fast food eaten in a pinch, she'd had left him swearing he wouldn't go there again. He had no idea how she'd found him, but he plastered a smile on his face and stood to greet her.

"There you are," she exclaimed in a voice meant to be heard by others.

"Scarlet," he said in an even voice, "what a pleasant surprise."

She strode over to his table in a huff. "Pleasant? Not at all. I'm here to tell you it's over between us. We're finished."

Kane raised a brow calmly, reasonably sure this show was not for his benefit. "I'm sorry to hear that."

"Sorry? You should be sorry, you bastard." She leaned in and snarled softly, "My publicist said you turned down my invitation to the San Diego gala. I'd already announced you would be there. Men don't turn me down; I turn them down. You understand?" She raised her voice again. "No, I don't care what you say, I'm not taking you back. Do you hear me? We're over. Now let go of my arm."

"I'm not touching you," Kane said dryly.

She pulled back from him as if he had been. "Don't beg. I won't change my mind." Even though he hadn't said a word, she said loudly, "How dare you!" She raised her hand as if to slap him in the face, but paused to look around. She pursed her lips and said in a low voice, "How could not one person have their phone out to take a picture of this? Do they know who I am?"

Kane flexed his shoulders and nodded at the familiar couple at the next table. Although the restaurant was well known, regulars also frequented it. The restaurant owner, Richard D'Argenson, had married into the Andrade family and in New York if you threw a stone, you were likely to hit one of them or someone who knew them. Gio had taken him there so many times, Kane had become comfortable and knew many of the people around him. "You chose your stage poorly if you were looking for publicity. I could probably kill someone here, and no one would say a word."

Scarlet's eyes rounded dramatically and she shrieked, "Are you threatening me?"

Kane rubbed a hand tiredly over his eyes and returned to his seat. "Enjoy the rest of your evening, Scarlet. Somewhere else."

Scarlet bent down near his ear. Her skin-tight red dress barely covered the tips of her breasts, but Kane felt nothing at the sight. "Every time you see me in a movie you'll think of what we had and what you'll never have again."

"I'm sure I will," Kane said with some irony.

"Asshole," she said, then flounced her way out of the restaurant.

Kane pinched the bridge of his nose wearily. A much softer female voice interrupted his moment of reprieve.

"Sorry I'm late."

Kane stood to greet Gio's wife, Julia, with a brief hug and a kiss to her cheek. She was the sweetest woman Kane had ever met and had a gentle, nurturing soul. When she'd called and asked Kane to meet with her privately, he hadn't hesitated to agree. Like anyone he considered family, he'd move heaven and earth for her. "Not late at all. I was just seated." He held out a chair for her.

Julia sat with a smile and wiggled happily in her chair. "I just saw Scarlet King in person. I wanted to ask her for her autograph, but she was out the door before I could. Richard must be so happy she came here to eat. Clients like that are good for business."

"Sometimes," Kane answered vaguely and retook his seat. He raised a hand and the waiter was instantly at the table. "What would you like to drink?"

Julia sat forward in her chair and with her hands tapping on the table in excitement. "I'll have a water this time. Can you guess why?"

After the waiter left, Kane answered, "Because you're thirsty?"

Julia's smile widened, if that was even possible. "No, because I'm pregnant. Gio and I are going to have a baby. Don't tell anyone, though. I want him to be able to share the news at our next Andrade dinner. And it's early, too early to make a formal announcement."

Kane reached across and gave her hand a warm, short squeeze. "I couldn't be happier for both of you. Congratulations."

"Thank you. A baby. We've been trying for years now, and I was starting to worry. So was Gio, even though he won't admit it. I can't tell you what this means for us. That is why Gio and I bought a place outside of the city; someplace big enough for my parents to come and stay with us and plenty of room for our growing family."

Two waters arrived and Kane took a substantial gulp. "Rena will feel the same when she and Nick get pregnant. My parents will be all over that."

"Children have a way of making the family you have even more important."

Kane nodded politely. "I imagine they do."

Julia put her hand on Kane's forearm. "That's why I've come to ask you for a favor. A really big one. I know how busy you are, but I hope you'll say yes."

"Whatever you need, Julia. You know that."

"It's not really for me, it's for Gio. It's something he needs that he'd never ask you for."

"Consider it done."

Plates of seafood crêpes arrived. Both Kane and Julia had eaten there often enough to know that regardless of what they ordered, Richard would send out what he considered his best that day. You didn't ask what you were going to get, and you didn't try to pay. Those were the rules of being someone Richard called family. It always amazed Kane how he kept his restaurants as profitable as they were.

"You know about his half-sister, Gigi."

"Of course."

"I know Leora asked us to back off and let her come to us, but I don't think that's going to ever happen. And no matter how happy Gio is about our life together and our baby, a part of him is still sad. I want to give him his sister back, and I'm asking you to help me."

Kane raised one eyebrow in surprise. "You want me to find her?"

"We know where she is," Julia answered sadly. "We've known for years. What we don't know is how to get her to believe her brothers want her in their lives. I can't even imagine growing up outside my family as she did. She must want to know them, but she shuts them out. She refuses to speak to them."

Gio had spoken of his sister often when he'd first discovered her, but when his attempts to meet with her had all been denied, he'd stopped mentioning her. Still, he couldn't see how he was the right choice to reach out to her. Shaking his head gently, Kane said, "Wouldn't you or someone from the Andrade clan have a better chance?"

Julia turned pleading eyes toward Kane. "I might have thought that once, but we've all tried. She puts a defensive wall up instantly. It's like she's so afraid of getting hurt she can't even hear what we say. Leora asked us to give Gigi a chance to come to us, but it has been years now. Maybe reaching out via someone who isn't emotionally involved would work."

Kane took a bite of his crêpe and used that time to think about what she was asking him to do. "You know I would do anything for Gio, but—"

Julia squeezed his forearm and continued to look up at him with the saddest puppy-dog eyes he'd ever seen. "I've seen you with Rena. You're a wonderful big brother. You also understand how important a sister can be. Gio wants Gigi to be happy, but he also wants to be a part of her life and for her to be a part of ours. Imagine if Rena wouldn't talk to you. How far would you go to try to repair that relationship?"

Kane nodded in understanding. As frustrating as she could sometimes be, he couldn't imagine his life without his sister. "Pretty damn far."

"Exactly. People tell him all the time to let it go. Let her go. But she's never agreed to meet with him, and that leaves everything unresolved. It's like that woman you used to ask about all the time. You don't talk about her anymore, but I bet it still weighs on you that you never found her, doesn't it?"

Kane frowned. "Not at all."

Julia sat back in her chair and shot him a knowing smile. "Of course not. Sorry, I don't even know why I brought her up."

"Me either."

"But you never did find her, did you?"

Kane pushed a piece of lobster around his plate. "No. No I didn't."

They ate in silence for the next few minutes. Kane's

thoughts drifted back to the night he'd met Luisella, and it filled him with the uneasiness he always felt when he thought of her. They had shared nothing more than a kiss and, as far as he was concerned, even that had been a lapse in good judgment. Still, no one he'd met before or since compared to her.

There were still times he considered hiring a private investigator to find her. He hadn't let himself go that far then and wasn't about to now.

Julia was right, though. He was haunted by questions that could only be answered by seeing her again. Would he want her as desperately as he had that night? Would the slightest touch from her still set his whole being on fire? Highly unlikely.

Especially after all this time. She might be married. With children. Looking for her now made no sense. But wanting to gave Kane an understanding of how a yearning didn't necessarily lessen over time. It could lay dormant, mostly denied, and still come robustly alive at the slightest query.

Luisella.

Fucking Luisella.

Julia placed her fork down on the side of her plate and asked gently, "Will you do it? Will you talk to Gigi? Try to convince her to meet her brothers? Make her see they love her, and they would have come for her sooner if they'd known she'd existed? I think she needs to hear that."

"I'll go see her," Kane said. "I'll explain what I know about the situation. That's all I can promise you."

"Bring her home, Kane. Or get her to agree to let us visit

her there. It would mean the world to Gio. And to me." Julia laid a hand across her still flat stomach. "Our baby has another aunt, and I want her to grow up knowing her."

"I can't force Gigi to do anything she doesn't want to, but I'll try, Julia. I'll rearrange my schedule and fly out to see her soon."

"I heard she'll be in Venice this weekend."

"This weekend? I'm committed to an event on Saturday."

Julia looked away, then back. "Stress is hard on a pregnancy, and waiting is very stressful."

Kane chuckled and threw his napkin on the table. "You did not just play the pregnancy card, did you?"

Julia smiled at him innocently. "Only if it worked."

Sighing in resignation, Kane said, "Send me all the information about where she'll be, and I'll fly over Friday night. Do you have recent photo of her?"

Julia dug through her purse. "I've had Alethea check up on her now and then." She pulled out a photo and handed it to Kane. "This picture was taken a couple weeks ago."

Kane accepted the photo, not knowing what to expect. He'd always assumed Gigi would look like a female version of Gio. He'd never actually given it much thought. He had to look at the photo twice before he believed what his eyes were telling him.

With a suddenly dry mouth, he demanded, "Who is this?"

Julia looked at him in confusion. "I told you, that's Gigi."

Every muscle in his body tightened painfully. Unfortunately, it was undeniably . . . *Luisella.*

Billions of people on the planet and the woman he couldn't forget just had to be his best friend's little sister.

Son of a bitch.

Chapter Five

SATURDAY MORNING GIGI woke and dressed early and headed toward the kitchen to make her mother an espresso. Ever since she was a child she'd brought her mother breakfast in bed as her birthday present.

The palazzo was just as it had been six months earlier and six months before that. The stone steps in the courtyard still needed weeding between the cracks. Another painting adorned a spot that had had been vacant for years. Gigi sent money to her mother each month so she wouldn't have to work so hard, but instead of lowering her workload her mother used the money to hunt down and repurchase items she'd sold off. Why couldn't her mother see that no matter how many pieces she bought back, it wouldn't change how the house felt—empty and sad. She should sell the place, but Gigi doubted she ever would. As supportive and loving as her mother was, she was stubborn in her own way.

On the way to the kitchen, Gigi stopped to pick up a new addition to her mother's framed photos. It was of her brother Luke with his wife, Cassie, and their little girl. Although Leora had said she understood when Gigi asked that they not talk about the Andrades anymore, it was obvious she'd stayed in contact with them. The constantly updated photos kept the topic open and painfully fresh at each visit.

You're killing me, Mamma. They're not even related to you. Why do you care about them?

Gigi considered herself a strong person. A levelheaded one. Most of her friends would describe her the same way. She was the one they came to for practical advice. They'd never seen the past pull her in like a powerful riptide, battering her with old insecurities and things she told herself no longer bothered her. Coming home always put her off-kilter.

It had been the same on Slater Island. She wasn't proud of any part of that trip. Her emotions had flopped back and forth so many times she hadn't been able to sort them out even after she'd returned home. She'd tried to box them up and put them aside with everything else unpleasant she couldn't change, but a deep sadness had lingered after her visit to the States.

She'd finally admitted to her mother she'd gone to the wedding. She'd deliberately left out certain details, but she did tell her mother that being around them made her sad in a way she couldn't handle. Another fact she wasn't proud of, but one her mother seemed to understand. Leora had kissed her daughter on the forehead and said, "Everything, even second chances, needs to come at the right time. Perhaps this is not it."

Her brothers had stopped trying to make contact after

that, and Gigi was able to put all of it out of her head and concentrate on starting a career. Which she had. She didn't want to look back. Not now. Not ever.

I should ignore these damn photos. She couldn't, though. They were in every room. Pictures of her brothers' weddings, their parties, their children being baptized. Even though Gigi had decided to not have contact with them, watching their lives continue on without her filled her with a different, but equally unwelcome, regret.

Shouldn't it get easier? Being in the home where her father had died, and then looking at photos of a family she didn't know always left her feeling raw and exposed. She didn't want to feel that way again. She didn't like the person she was when she visited this house.

She replaced the photo on the mantel and told herself to think of it like a canker sore . . . no matter how bad it feels in the moment, it doesn't last, and the pain is quickly forgotten.

Two days. I'm only here for two days; then it's back to my life in Scotland.

Back to sanity.

She was gathering some pastries onto a tray when she heard a knock at the door. Gigi rushed to answer it, expecting a birthday delivery of some sort. She whipped open the door and gasped. Right on her doorstep was the one man she'd never forgotten, and the last one she wanted to see.

Kane.

Here.

Oh, God.

He was dressed in a button-down dark blue shirt and trousers, but he was every bit as sexy as he'd been in a tuxedo. Her heart started thudding wildly in her chest. Every inch of her came alive in a way it didn't for other men. She licked her bottom lip as her mind went blissfully blank. This was the zing she'd told Annelise she was holding out for.

"May I come in?" His voice was deep and strong.

"What do you want?" Gigi asked in a whisper.

It was impossible to look away from his eyes, impossible to miss how her question had lit a fire within him. At least that was what Gigi thought until he said, "Your family sent me."

Gigi's breath left her in a rush. She was instantly angry, and although she didn't want to admit it, disappointed. "I'm sorry, but I'm not interested in anything they have to say." She went to close the door, but he put out a hand to stop her.

"Not everything is about you. It's time to stop hiding, *Luisella*."

Gigi's face went hot with a blush. "I'm not hiding." She gave the door a slight push, but he held it firmly in place. "And I don't have to explain myself to you."

"Who's at the door, Gigia?" Leora called from the stairway.

"No one," Gigi answered over her shoulder and gave the door another shove. "Just a salesman peddling something we don't want."

"Oh, I was hoping it was . . ." Leora's voice rose happily when she saw who her daughter was blocking from entering.

She paid no attention to the obvious battle ensuing and said, "Kane! Come in. Julia told me you might drop by."

"Leora, it's a pleasure to finally meet you." The smug look he shot Gigi made her want to slam the door in his face, but her mother was already at her side, welcoming him.

"I've heard so many stories about you through Gio that I feel I know you. Come in. You must be tired from traveling. Gigia, could you make some espresso for everyone?"

Gigi let the door swing wide open. "I'd love to," she answered with heavy sarcasm.

Kane stepped inside and gave her mother a quick kiss on each cheek. "I hope I'm not intruding."

Her mother dismissed the idea with a wave of her hand. "Company is the best birthday present."

Kane met Gigi's eyes, but directed his next comment to her mother. "I'm here to take Gigi back to the United States to meet her brothers."

"I know," her mother said, sounding pleased with the idea. "Do you think you're up to the task?"

Gigi's mouth fell open in shock. "Do either of you care that I can hear you?"

Kane turned his attention back to Leora as if Gigi hadn't spoken. "When I set my mind to do something, I never fail."

"It won't be easy," Leora warned with a demure smile.

"I don't expect it to be, but she is coming with me."

Finding her voice again, Gigi said, "Have the two of you lost your minds? I'm not going anywhere. And, Kane, if there was the slightest chance I was going to talk to you at all, you just blew it."

"Gigia," her mother scolded softly. "Where are you manners? Please go make the espresso."

With an infuriating slight smile on his face, Kane said, "Gigia, what a beautiful name."

Standing straighter, Gigi inhaled sharply. "Don't call me that. My name is Gigi."

"Gigia," her mother scolded again, then turned and linked arms with Kane, leading him toward the parlor. "It's a good thing you're here, Kane. She could use a strong influence in her life. Since my Gio died, she's been lost, and I thought if I gave her time she would find her way back. But I don't know what to do with her anymore."

Gigi stood just where they'd left, replaying the last few minutes in her head. Why would her brothers send a friend instead of coming for her themselves? And why were her mother and a man she'd met only once in her life talking about her as if they were on the same side?

In all of her life no man had ever spoken to her as arrogantly as Kane had. She hated to admit how hearing him talk that way had sent flames of desire licking through her. He was a man who knew what he wanted and would stop at nothing to get it.

And he wanted her.

Although, not the way she was picturing.

No, this is just my luck. Mr. Zing finally arrives, and all he wants to do is lecture me again.

✧   ✧   ✧

KANE SAT WITH Leora in the parlor making polite conversation, but all he could think about was how seeing Lui—Gigi—had felt.

He remembered everything, right down to his desire to throw all sense to the wind and fuck her without regard for consequence or loyalty. He wouldn't, of course. At the end of the day she was his best friend's little sister and would always be off limits, but that didn't make whatever was between them less powerful.

He groaned inwardly as he remembered how he'd spoken to her. On the long flight over, he'd planned a much more diplomatic approach. He'd chosen his words carefully, mentally outlined how he would guide her toward agreeing to go back with him. In his head, he'd imagined a civil conversation.

Not the he-man, chest-pounding I'm-taking-you-back-to-the-States-whether-you-fight-me-or-not declaration he'd made.

His mother would have boxed him in the ears if she ever heard him speak that way. He would have done worse had he heard someone speak that way to his sister. Still, something had snapped within him when she'd moved to close the door in his face.

Something primal and wild.

He had come for her, and he'd decided in that moment he wasn't leaving without her. She would fly back to meet her brothers, and he would take whatever he felt around her and deny, deny, deny the shit out of it.

That's what men do when their cock decides it likes their best friend's sister.

"Do you have a plan?" Leora asked, bringing Kane back to their conversation.

It was odd talking about it with Gigi's mother, and Kane gave her a guilty, somewhat sheepish, smile. "Not really."

Leora smiled, and he could see where Gigi's beauty came from. Even in her sixties, she was elegant, stunning. It should have surprised him that she was on his side, but it matched what Gio and Julia had told him about her. Fiercely loyal to her daughter and the memory of the man she'd loved. "I like you, Kane. You're strong. My Gio was like you. He didn't make excuses for who he was, but when he loved, he loved with all his heart. Gigia needs to forgive him. She sees everything as good or bad. Forgivable or inexcusable. It's not good for her. I live my life the best I can and leave the judging up to God. I don't think Gigia will ever be happy until she learns to do the same."

Kane nodded, but only because he wasn't sure what to say in the face of such raw honesty.

"And she's stubborn, my Gigia. Just like her father. She misses him still, you know. It's why she hates coming here. She thinks I don't understand, but I do. It's why I make her come here ever year for my birthday. I miss him, too, and I will not let him be forgotten. He loved us too much for me to let that happen."

Kane looked away, moved by Leora's words and uncomfortable at the same time. He didn't want to see Gigi as someone who needed him. After he convinced her to see her brothers, it was his intention to never see her again. He cleared his throat and brought the subject back to a safer topic. "Gigia is a beautiful name. Why doesn't she use it?"

"She doesn't want to be Venetian. Sometimes I think she doesn't want to be my daughter. I don't know which breaks my heart more. When I was child I used to make wishes on candles and keep them secret, believing that only then would they come true. I have learned since that very little happens if you don't make it known. Please convince my Gigia to go with you to the States. She needs to know her brothers. And if I can impose one additional request—bring her back to me one day. All the way back, as my proud little Venetian." Leora wiped a tear from her cheek and reached for a tissue. "I'm sorry. I'm making you uncomfortable."

Kane leaned forward and took one of Leora's hands in his, giving it a gentle squeeze. He was both touched and overwhelmed by her request. Yes, his family often fearlessly got involved before their assistance was requested, but not with anything on this scale. "If it were in my power, I would do both for you today. I'll do my best to get her back to the States. That's all I can promise."

Leora sniffed and gave his hand a pat. "Thank you." She stood. "I'm going to retire to my room now. Good luck with my daughter, Kane." She walked to the door and stopped just before it, looking back over her shoulder as she said, "And tell Julia she chose well."

Chapter Six

GIGI SLAMMED THREE espresso cups onto the tray with the pastries. If her mother hadn't been there she would have told him exactly where he could go.

And why hadn't her mother told her he was coming? After Kane left, and he would be leaving soon, she would have a talk with her mother. She knew Gigi didn't like surprises.

Of course, to Mamma, he's only Gio's friend, here to try to sway me into changing my mind. She doesn't know about the added layer of humiliation I felt at his rejection . . . that he is the only man I've thrown myself at, only to be laughed off.

Stings like that linger.

Gigi considered leaving, taking a water taxi and hopping on the next flight home. She didn't have to stick around and be spoken about as if she were an errant child. She was a successful businesswoman. People respected her opinion. She didn't need to prove herself here.

It's time stop hiding, Luisella. Kane's words replayed in her head.

Gigi picked up the tray and straightened her shoulders. *I'm not hiding, and no one can make me do anything I don't want to do. I'll be nice to Kane for Mamma's benefit, then send him on his way.*

She pushed the swinging kitchen door open with one hip. *And I'll do it calmly, gracefully. Because I am not the emotional wreck he met three years ago.*

Not that I care what he thinks of me.

Gigi stopped at the doorway of the parlor. Kane stood at her arrival, but he was alone.

"Your mother said she was tired and retired to her room."

Gigi forced herself to start walking again. She placed the tray on a table in front of one of the settees. "I'll check on her after you leave, but for now, please sit." *See? Perfectly civilized and in control.*

Kane took a seat beside the tray and watched her intently while he took a long sip. "Ah, nothing like Italian espresso. It's different back home." He replaced the cup on the tray and sat back. "However, it's not what I'm here for."

Gigi stood behind one of the chairs. She felt like a hare caught in the sights of a wolf. It was exciting even though she had no intention of going with him or bolting. "I appreciate that you've come a long way to speak with me. I'm sorry to say, though, you've wasted your time."

He raised an eyebrow, but didn't seem put-off by her statement. "Not a waste at all, I had to come here to understand you. You're a liar, little Gigia."

Gigi opened her mouth to deny it, then answered shortly, "Once. One lie."

Kane stood and approached her. "Hardly. I'm sure I

wasn't the only person you lied to that day."

"Only because I didn't want people to know I was there."

He continued to speak while walking toward her. "Why would anyone sneak into a wedding they'd been invited to?"

Gigi gripped the back of the chair with one hand. "I was curious, that's all."

Stopping just inches away, Kane loomed above her. "Another lie. They fall from your lips so easily. I wonder if you believe them yourself."

With Kane so close, Gigi was finding it difficult to concentrate on anything besides the breadth of his shoulders and the lure of his dark eyes. She gulped. "Get out of my house."

He ran a hand lightly down one of her cheeks. "When I leave, you're coming with me. Tell me, Gigi, do you still swear like a sailor?"

Mesmerized by his voice, it was impossible to be offended by his words. Her lips parted involuntarily, and she raised her chin. "You deserved what I said."

Kane rubbed a thumb across her bottom lip. "Did I? Because I refused you?"

Pride warred with common sense. If he couldn't even remember how she'd embarrassed herself that evening, did reminding him of it serve any purpose except to embarrass herself again? She needed to back away from him, forget about the incident that had apparently not meant much to him. "Because you laughed when you did."

He took her chin in his hand and held her face so he could look down into her eyes. "Is that what you thought? If

I laughed, it was at myself for not realizing how young you were."

Gigi gulped again. Three years was a long time. The feel of his kiss shouldn't be so easy to remember. It wasn't as if she hadn't dated anyone since. When she'd first moved to Scotland she'd gone to dinner with several men. Her pride had been hurt, and she'd had something to prove to herself. But she hadn't slept with anyone of them.

This is why.

Sorry, Annelise, you were wrong. The zing was, unfortunately, very real.

There were so many things she wanted to say to him, but they didn't matter in that moment. She was lost in his touch, his gaze, in the tantalizing scent of him. "I was twenty-two, not a child."

He dropped his hand and stepped back. "Just because something isn't legally wrong, doesn't make it right."

His withdrawal hurt even though she told herself it was what she wanted. "Can we stop talking about the past? I'd rather forget it."

Kane's eyes flashed with a challenge. "Would you?"

Gigi glared at him. "I don't like you."

His smile was twisted with irony. "That's probably for the best, but not why I'm here. I know why you went to the wedding even if you're not brave enough to tell me."

Gigi pursed her lips in irritation, and glared at a place halfway up his chest.

"You want to know your brothers, but you're too damn scared to get out of your own way and let it happen."

"I'm not—" She stopped before voicing the lie. "Even if I am, who are you to come here and judge me? You don't know me. You don't know what I've been through. I went to that damn wedding in a moment of weakness, and it didn't make it better. It made it worse. What you call hiding, I call making healthy choices. If I know something hurts me, why would I do it again? I have a life in Scotland where I am perfectly happy. I have a career I love. Tell me, why I should risk that?"

Frowning, Kane softened his voice. "You really are scared."

Gigi turned away. She'd already told him more than she'd meant to. More than she'd ever said to anyone.

His voice was gentle and from a spot right behind her. "Do you know why I'm here?"

Without turning, Gigi answered tightly, "For my brothers." She didn't add the part that hurt even though it was ridiculous. *Not for me. He wouldn't come for me.*

"Gio's wife, Julia, actually. She's pregnant, and she wants you in her child's life."

"I'm sorry, but—"

With a hand on her arm, Kane swung Gigi around. "You're not sorry at all. Julia is one of the kindest, sweetest women I know. You're lucky she cares enough about you to send anyone for you."

Gigi struggled against his hold. "Lucky? Which part of this should I feel good about? The fact that no one respects my wishes to be left alone or your manhandling?"

His nostrils flared and his hand tightened on her arm

before he released her roughly. "You're three years older, but you haven't changed at all from the angry little girl I met on Slater Island."

"And you're still as condescending and full of yourself."

They stood there, nose to nose, in a heavily charged stand off.

From the doorway, Leora chastised both of them. "The two of you could wake the dead with your arguing." She walked into the room, took a seat, and picked up her espresso. "I was hoping your talk would go better."

Kane shook his head, folding his arms across his chest arrogantly. "She's impossible."

Gigi folded her arms in a similar fashion and planted her feet stubbornly. "Me? Mamma, I told him to leave, but he's too thickheaded to go."

Keeping his eyes on Gigi's, Kane growled, "I'll leave the moment you agree to go with me and not before."

Gigi leaned in and growled back, "Then I hope you enjoy sleeping in my mother's parlor because I'm not going anywhere with you."

"Gigia," Leora said in a softly authoritative tone, "come sit with me."

Reluctantly, Gigi backed away from Kane and went to sit beside her mother. Leora took one of her hands between both of hers and held it on her lap. "When you said you wanted to go to school in England, did I stop you?"

"No, Mamma," Gigi said. She knew just how much her mother had given up for her and although she could fight with the rest of the world, she could never fight with someone who loved her as her mother did.

"And when you wanted to go to the university there, I agreed you should do what you want, didn't I? We made it happen together, didn't we?"

"Yes."

"I would do anything for you. I couldn't love you more, but that doesn't mean I agree with your choices. You're wrong on this, Gigia. So very wrong. Life goes by in a flash. Do you really want to miss your chance to know your family? To be one of them?"

"I have a family. I have you."

Leora gave Gigi a gentle smile. "You have so much more. Go back with Kane. Meet your brothers and their wives. If you don't like them, we'll never talk of them again. But don't shut your heart to love unless you're given a good reason to."

Gigi shook her head back and forth as she absorbed her mother's request. "So, what would you have me do—go back with him now? Just like that? I have a business to run. I have commitments."

Leora met her daughter's eyes. "You have a partner. She'll understand. Go, Gigia. Do this for me."

Gigi looked across the room at Kane. His expression was unreadable. Their eyes met. Was Kane really there because her sister-in-law was pregnant and wanted to meet her? *Why is my mother so determined that I meet the very people who turned their backs on her?* She thought back to the way her brothers had looked at their wives with love and tenderness. Why had they denied Gigi and her mother as long as they did? They claimed they wanted to know Gigi now. Words that came too late. Empty claims that meant nothing more than all the promises their father had made. None of that changed the hopeful look on her mother's face. If going to the States put an end to her mother worrying over the topic, then let it be so.

"I'll go."

Kane's smile held approval and a touch of satisfaction as if he'd personally convinced her.

Gigi added, "Only because you asked me to, Mamma. Not for any other reason."

⟡ ⟡ ⟡

SEVERAL HOURS LATER, Kane sat across from Gigi in the lounge area of his private jet. She hadn't said more than yes or no to him since they'd left Venice. Normally he would have appreciated a quiet flight since he had emails to answer and project proposals to read. He'd taken out his laptop and tried to work, but his attention kept drifting back to the woman who was nervously chewing her thumbnail as she stared out the window. He said, "I spoke with Julia. She and Gio will meet us when we land."

Gigi didn't acknowledge she'd heard him.

"When you first meet Gio you may think he's standoffish. He doesn't mean to be. Once you get to know him, he's actually quite funny."

In a quiet voice, Gigi said, "He came to my mother's house after my father died. He was there to bring Papa back to the States. He threatened my mother, threatened to take our home if she ever spoke of my father. That's all I will see when I look at him."

"He didn't know about you then, Gigi."

"So he claims."

"I grew up with Gio. He's like a brother to me. If he says he didn't know, I believe him."

With her face still averted, Gigi said, "Either way, he was cruel to my mother. I can't forgive that, even if she can."

Kane put his laptop aside. "When I first met Gio I teased him about taking everything too seriously. It wasn't until we became good friends I realized how a family could look normal from the outside but be completely dysfunctional. Gio's mother passed away nearly four years ago, but her legacy lives on in her sons. She did everything she could to set them against each other. I'm not defending what you heard Gio say that day, but I can make a good guess why he said it. He was a messenger, Gigi, and a young one. Don't hold that day against him."

Gigi looked across at Kane tentatively. "What did he say when you told him I was coming?"

"He said, 'Good.'"

"That's it?"

"That's Gio."

"You said his wife, Julia, is a nice woman?"

"The nicest. So sweet you'll wonder if it's an act, but after you spend enough time with her you'll see she is completely genuine."

Gigi looked at, then hid, her chewed nail beneath her other hand. "She seemed to be a good match for him when I saw them together."

"She is. They bring out the best in each other."

"Are you close to all of them—my brothers? What are they like?"

She asked the question with such yearning his heart went out to her. He wanted to gather her into his arms and reassure her everything would be fine, her brothers would love her, and that coming was indeed the right decision. He wanted to swear he'd stay with her to ensure it all worked out. He couldn't. Being so close to her would be its own sweet torture. After he handed her off to Gio, he needed to put as much distance as he could between them. What had initially been a purely physical attraction was deepening. Watching Gigi with her mother had shown him another side of her. She wasn't childishly defiant, as he'd originally thought. She felt hurt and rejected by her brothers and dealt with those feelings by isolating herself. She needed a bridge back to her brothers. "Gio is the oldest. As I said, he takes his role very seriously. Luke is the second oldest. At first, you'll probably like him the best. I've never met a person who didn't get along with Luke. He has an easy way about him. He was a surgeon in New York, but now he practices in Ohio. He and his wife, Cassie have a two-and-a-half-year-old. She's a hoot. I joke that she has a lot of Nick in her, and if that's true she's going to give her parents a run for their money. Nick married my sister, Rena. They don't have any children yet, thank God. I'm not sure the world is ready for their offspring. Nick is . . . irreverent. He was a hard one to like until my sister fell in love with him. Don't take anything he says seriously. He has a sense of humor that can take a while to get used to. The youngest is Max. He married Tara. Max has always done his own thing, so of the four I know him the least, but he's been spending a lot more time with his family since he and his wife had their first child last Christmas."

"You make them sound like regular people."

"What do you think they are?"

Gigi's eyes were wide with emotion. "I'm not like them. I wasn't raised with money. I'm proud of what I do, but I didn't grow up like this." She referenced the jet with a wave of her hand.

"What exactly do you do?"

"I connect people who have something to sell with either an auction house or a private buyer. It's a business my friend Annelise and I sort of fell into after college. I knew my mother had sold off items to pay for my schooling, but it wasn't until I heard her speaking to a friend about the process that I realized how often she'd been taken advantage of. Her friend, Doris Sneddon, was looking to sell off some estate items to stop her family home from going into foreclosure. Doris lived just outside of Edinburgh. Annelise was from that area, so I asked her to help me help Doris. We catalogued her estate and helped her sell the least number of items for the most amount of money. Word of mouth is a powerful thing. Money was tight in the beginning, but we've had a constant stream of clients since. We compare it to running a funeral home. No one wants to come to us, but we make the best of difficult situations, and people are grateful for that." As Gigi spoke about her life in Edinburgh, her nervousness fell away. She was once again the confident woman he remembered from their first meeting. There was passion in her voice as she spoke about what she did for a living. Kane could have listened to her speak for hours. Still, something she'd said bothered him. "Your father was a wealthy man. He didn't leave you anything in his will?" Kane's temper rose at the thought of how little it would have taken on her father's part to ensure his mistress and child were taken care of. That was something he'd speak to Gio about the first opportunity he had.

Gigi tensed again. "I believe he left Mamma the palazzo, but that's all. I've never seen the official paperwork, so I don't know if it's legally ours. I don't like to think about the possibility that it might not be. It would break my mother's heart if she lost it now."

"You'll never have to worry about money again, Gigi."

Gigi's head snapped around, and her eyes flashed with anger. "I'm not here for a handout."

Kane raised one hand in a call for peace. "No one said you were, but your brothers will want to make sure you have what you need."

Gigi's cheeks reddened with temper. "My mother made sure I wanted for nothing, and now I work hard to make sure she has the same. Neither one of us require charity."

Her beautiful chin jutting out proudly and her eyes bright with emotion left Kane momentarily speechless. The depth of how much he cared about the outcome of this visit shook him. He'd like to believe the protective feeling he felt for her was because she was Gio's little sister, but it was unfortunately more complicated than that.

"Gigi, it's not charity if you're family."

She pressed her lips angrily together, and he decided to let the topic drop for a while. He looked at his watch. They'd touch down on a private landing strip outside New York City in a couple hours. "You should sleep if you can. It'll be a long day otherwise."

She took a blanket off the seat beside her and tucked it around her legs. "I wanted to book a hotel room, but Julia insisted I stay with them in their new house."

There it was again, that uncertainty that made him crave to be her champion. *Bringing her back is more than anyone else has been able to do. Let that be enough.* "That sounds like Julia. You'll be fine there."

"Will you—will you be there?"

Even though everything in him wanted to say he would, he couldn't lie to her. "No. You won't see me again after today. At least, not during this visit."

He caught a glimpse of sadness in her eyes before she nodded, hitched the blanket up higher, and turned to look back out the window. "I didn't want to come."

"I know," he said gently.

"But I guess it was time. Thank you, Kane, for not leaving when I tried to slam the door in your face."

"Get some sleep, Gigi."

Kane picked his laptop up and opened it, but his thoughts were not on the work awaiting him. He didn't consider himself an emotional man, but when it came to the woman across from him he was all tangled up inside.

Right and wrong were impossible to distinguish from each other. He hated sounding like he was depositing then deserting her, but that was exactly what he needed to do. He was already beyond being able to be with her and pretend he felt nothing. He ached for Gigi in a gloriously painful way.

Her closed eyes gave him the opportunity to study her delicate features, the curve of her long neck, and the sweet outline of her breasts where the blanket had fallen away. He doubted she was actually sleeping, but he wouldn't call her bluff. The less they spoke the better.

He could already feel himself falling for the one woman he would never allow himself to have.

Gio's little sister. *Keep telling yourself that, Kane. Gio's little sister.*

Chapter Seven

Maybe it was because she had anticipated meeting her brothers for so long that she was an emotional basket case, but Gigi was unable to sleep. After a brief, fitful attempt at a nap, Gigi opened her eyes and said, "Kane?"

Kane looked up from working on his laptop. "Yes?"

"I can't sit here and pretend I'm not going crazy on the inside, but I don't want to talk about my family or the past."

Kane shut his computer and put it off to the side. "Okay. Have you ever been to the States before?" Before she had a chance to say anything, he said, "Besides Slater Island."

"No," Gigi said slowly. Her father hadn't taken her anywhere but she couldn't say that nor did she want to think about it. "I haven't had a reason to. I travel around Europe for my job. Mostly I get to dig through people's dusty attics, but I love exploring new towns. How about you? Do you travel much?"

"Like you, only for work." Kane made a slightly dissatisfied face. "I took over my family's company a couple years ago and it's pretty much taken me over as well."

"What kind of business is it?"

"It's diversified developments. That's a fancy way of saying we follow the money. Whether it needs to be torn down, built, maintained, or dug up we have the resources around the globe to make it happen. A lot of what we do is for governments, but I've been expanding into the private sector, and the opportunities are limitless there."

"Sounds exciting."

"It is. My father built the company and a strong reputation, so really all I had to do was not fuck it up. But I wanted to prove to him that I could do as well as he had, and that meant taking it to the next level."

Gigi loved the warmth in Kane's eyes as he talked about his father. "You sound very close."

"We are," Kane said simply. "I have a small family. Mostly just my parents and my sister, but not much happens to any of us that the others don't instantly know about. That can be both a blessing and a curse. If I miss a family dinner there is hell to pay."

Gigi clasped her hands on her lap. "I can't imagine that. My mother and I are more friends, I guess, than mother and daughter. We have our own lives. We check in with each other now and then, but it's nothing like your family sounds."

Kane looked across at her intently. "My impression was she loves you very much."

Gigi nodded slowly. "I know she does. We're just very different people." Thinking about how often she'd tried and failed to connect with her mother threatened to make Gigi sad, and that wasn't a layer of emotion she was looking to add to her already frayed nerves. "How did you break your nose?"

Kane's hand went to the bridge of his nose, and a large smile spread across his face. "I would like to say college football, but I accidentally dated a married woman once. I probably could have blocked the punch, but part of me felt I deserved it."

"How do you accidentally date a married woman?"

Kane laughed. "Start with the underdeveloped frontal lobe of an adolescent boy, add alcohol, and a trip to Montana. I hired her for ski lessons, but I learned a lot more than that before her husband showed up."

"You were a teenager?"

"Nineteen," Kane said with an unabashed smile. "Old enough to appreciate the lessons, but too young to notice her ring."

"You're right. You did deserve that punch."

He folded his arms across his chest and challenged, "Are you trying to tell me all of your choices have been good ones?"

"No," Gigi said with a chuckle and was surprised at how easily she and Kane had fallen into a comfortable conversation. "You're right. We all make mistakes. Was that your worst?"

"So far," Kane said cryptically and excused himself, claiming he needed to make a few phone calls. When he returned they continued to talk, but their topics remained much less personal.

When the pilot requested they prepare for landing, Gigi

discovered she didn't want her time with Kane to end. The first time she'd met him, she'd thought he was arrogant and harsh. At her mother's house, she'd dismissed him as an overconfident ass. She'd desperately wanted to get away from him.

Now as the plane touched down, Gigi couldn't deny how good she felt around Kane. Not just because she was attracted to him, but also because he made her laugh. Meeting her family for the first time wasn't scary with him at her side. He made her feel safe . . . *and* confused as all hell.

Every time he looked at her, her chest would tighten; her inner muscles would quiver. His voice was as sexy as the rest of him. His brief overview of East Coast weather patterns had her wet and ready for him as if he were whispering indecent proposals into her ear. She craved him in a way that defied logic.

And he's not even into me.

Or is he?

There were a few times during the flight she'd caught him watching her, and she let herself imagine it was lust she saw in his eyes. Her body would warm deliciously in response, and then he would say something completely impersonal, leaving her to wonder if he'd been looking at her or through her as he thought about something else.

When they'd stood nose to nose in her mother's parlor, Gigi could have sworn the air had sizzled with mutual sexual attraction, but there'd been no evidence of it since. He'd as much as told her he'd be happy with never seeing her again.

Kane stood when the plane came to a halt and held out

his hand to her. "Are you ready?"

She placed her hand in his and joined him, savoring the desire that shot through her, since it might be the last time she felt it. "Not really, but it's too late to turn back now."

He frowned as if conflicted about something, then took out a business card and held it out to her. "Take my card."

Gigi gasped in surprise. Did this mean what she thought it did? Was he saying he would leave it to her to make the first move? She accepted the card with a shaky hand. If she were smart she'd toss it out as she had the one she'd received from the creepy redhead when she was twenty-two. Some numbers were best not called.

But, oh, Kane would be a mistake worth making.

His next words were an embarrassing slap of reality. "It's my pilot's number. You're not trapped here. I'm sure you won't need the option, but if you do, the plane's there for you."

Letting out a long, slow breath, Gigi hoped her face had not revealed any of the rollercoaster she'd just taken herself on. Her only saving grace was she tended not to share her thoughts aloud. She plastered a grateful smile on her face. "Thank you."

The pilot opened the jet door and lowered the stairs. Kane put out his hand and said, "After you."

Once clear of the jet door, Gigi saw Gio and Julia standing beside a black limo. Gio's expression was hidden by sunglasses. Julia's bright smile competed with the sunshine. Gigi hesitated, gripping the railing tightly with one hand. *This is it.* They'd either welcome her as she'd always dreamed they would, or reveal an alternate reason they wanted to meet her. *Either way, no more hiding.*

From behind her, Kane said softly, "You're stronger than you think, Gigi."

Gigi nodded. She put a brave smile on her face and slowly made her way toward her eldest brother.

Julia rushed forward, smiling and crying at the same time. She threw her arms around Kane. "You did it. I knew you would."

Kane said something that Gigi missed as her attention swiveled to Gio. He was intimidatingly tall with stern features. Gigi had only two real memories of him, and they swirled through her: one from the day he threatened her mother and the other from his wedding. She held out her hand to shake his and raised her eyes to his. *Please be the man I saw at your wedding.*

He took off his sunglasses and looked her over, leaving her standing there with her hand awkwardly held out to him. Gigi lowered it, confused, and took a step back. *I knew this was a mistake.*

Julia was beside her in an instant. "Gigi, you don't know how much it means to us that you're here. You can tell me no, but may I hug you? I am bursting with the need to."

Numb from Gio's rejection, Gigi nodded absently. Julia threw her arms around her and practically strangled her in her enthusiasm. When Julia pulled back, she was beaming. It was impossible not to instantly love her for her welcome.

Julia bounded over to her husband. "Just hug her, Gio. I know you want to."

Gio stepped toward his sister. Gigi held her ground, refusing to retreat again. He pulled her to him for what was the most awkward hug she'd ever received. He was as tense as she was. She drew back and took another look at his face. Was it possible he was nervous, too? She noted a shine to his eyes that he blinked back, and she felt tears fill her own.

Over her head, he said, "Kane, thank you."

Kane cleared his throat. "You're welcome."

Gio released Gigi. "I've waited a long time for this day."

"Me, too," Gigi whispered. "Me, too."

Julia chirped in, "I'm sure you both have a lot of catching up to do, but let's do it at home." She turned to Kane. "Are you coming for dinner?"

Gigi swung around to see Kane point to a sedan that had just pulled up behind the limo. "Not this time, Julia. I have a lot of work to catch up on, and my ride is here."

"Tomorrow night?" Julia asked hopefully.

Kane shook his head. "My schedule is packed for the next couple of weeks. But I'll give you a call."

Gigi met Kane's eyes and, for just a moment, she would have sworn she saw sadness there, but she decided she was simply superimposing her desires onto him.

It had been impossible to forget him after meeting him at the wedding.

This time, she wouldn't even try. She mouthed, "Goodbye."

He stood there with an expression she couldn't decipher, then nodded, and strode to his car.

Inside the limo, with Julia happily describing the house

she and Gio had purchased outside the city, Gigi turned to watch Kane's car pull away.

⋄   ⋄   ⋄

Kane sat at the desk in his home office and instead of turning his computer on, he poured himself a Scotch and downed it in one gulp. He was pouring himself a second when his cell phone rang. He checked the caller ID. Rena. His sister must have heard he'd returned with Gigi and wanted the scoop.

Shit.

He answered curtly. "I'm working tonight, Rena. What do you want?"

Not one to be easily offended, his tone didn't ruffle Rena at all. "There's my sweet brother. Take a minute out of your plan for world domination and let me do something that will surely shock you. I'm calling to tell you how amazing you are. I can't believe you were able to do what everyone else failed at. You have to tell me how you got Gigi to agree to come back with you."

Kane downed his second Scotch in one swig. "I'd love to give you the slow-motion replay, but it really wasn't that exciting. She wants to know her brothers as much as they want to know her. All I did was give her a nudge."

Rena was quiet for a moment. "What's wrong?"

"Nothing."

"Something happened. I can hear it in your voice."

"What you hear is a man who put off several meetings to fly off to Venice only to fly back the next day. I'm happy it all worked out, but I'm tired, and I have things I need to get done before I can go to bed, so I'm irritable. Can we have this conversation tomorrow?"

"If that's what you want," Rena said slowly.

"It's exactly what I want."

"Hey, one last thing. Julia invited all of us over for dinner tomorrow. Do you want to drive over with us?"

Kane closed his eyes and rubbed the bridge of his nose in frustration. "I'm not going. This week is a busy one for me."

"What do you mean you're not going? How many times do we celebrate something like this? Come on, Kane, whatever you're working on can be put off for one night. You have to come—"

"I said no." Kane's tone was harsher than he meant it to be.

"Okay, that's it. Now I know something's wrong. You can either tell me or I'm driving over there. Your choice."

It might have been the alcohol or the fatigue that loosened Kane's tongue, but he said, "Gigi is Luisella. Or Luisella is Gigi." He poured himself another drink. "However the fuck you want to say it."

"Who?" Rena asked, then her voice rose as she remembered the name. "Oh, Luisella. The woman from the wedding."

"Yeah. Exactly."

"Are you sure?"

Kane made a pained noise as his answer.

"Oh, that sucks, Kane. Or that's great. I mean, you found her, but—"

"But I could never do that to Gio."

"It could work out. Look at Nick and me."

Kane took another swig of Scotch. "Nick. I nearly killed him when I found out. There are certain things you don't do to another man. You don't sleep with his wife, and you don't fuck his little sister."

"Are you drinking?" Rena asked.

"Yes, and I'm just getting started."

"Do you want me to come over?"

"No."

"I'm calling Dad." With that Rena hung up.

And Kane let out a very long, string of expletives.

Chapter Eight

Gigi had unpacked her things into a room the size of her apartment in Edinburgh. When Julia had described their new home, she'd left out that it was practically a castle with enough winding hallways to easily get lost. The homes on Slater Island had been impressive, but this was American opulence.

When Gigi had first stepped out of the car and looked at the sheer size of the building, her jaw had dropped. Julia had noticed and said quickly, "It seems like too much house at first, but you'd be surprised how quickly it fills up."

Gigi had looked around doubtfully. "I can't imagine."

"You won't have to," Julia had assured her. "You'll see tomorrow night. I hope you don't mind, but I invited some of the family over to meet you."

What could Gigi say to that? She'd thanked Julia and asked to see her room to freshen up. In the mirror of her bedroom, Gigi had given herself a stern talking to. Of course Julia had invited the family to come to meet her. There was nothing wrong with that. She hadn't come all this way to keep hiding. She eventually had to meet the family, why not over a dinner tomorrow?

Kane's words echoed in her head. "You're stronger than you think." *He's right. I'm not running away this time. I need to do this.*

She left her room and headed downstairs to find Julia.

"Gigi, I'd like to speak to you for a moment." Gio stood at the door of what looked like his study.

"Of course," Gigi said.

Gio led her to a pair of settees and motioned for her to sit. She did, but he continued to stand. "How is your room?"

"Lovely," Gigi answered in awkward politeness. She couldn't help adding, "Huge."

A small smile pulled at Gio's lips. "I'm glad. I want you to be comfortable here."

Is this where I'm supposed to lie and say I am? "Thank you."

"There are things you need to know, things you would have heard before now if you had been willing to speak with any of us."

Gigi stood, rising as her temper did. "Don't speak to me like I'm a child."

"Sit down," Gio commanded as if he were indeed addressing one.

Gigi remained standing and squared her shoulders. "No. I'm fine the way I am. Say whatever it is you want me to hear."

Running a hand through his hair, Gio looked irritated by her defiance. "You don't have to turn this into a confrontation."

"Yes, I do. We both know you have an ugly side. I'm just warning you I am not the kind of person who responds well to intimidation or your patronizing tone."

"An ugly side? What the hell are you talking about?"

Old anger surfaced with memories. For a moment, Gigi was eavesdropping from behind the shutters of the palazzo. What she'd held back for so long spilled out. "I heard you with my mother after our father died. I know what you said to her because I was there. So you can pretend to care about me, but I know you're not sincere. Why do you really want to meet me, Gio?"

"You were there?" Gio asked, going pale. "I didn't know. I didn't even know you existed."

With a chest tight with anger, Gigi let out what she'd held in for so long. "But if you had, things would have been different? I don't believe that. My father used to tell me stories about you and your brothers—"

"Your brothers, too," Gio said tightly.

Gigi continued as if he hadn't spoken. "He said you would accept me, but that wasn't what I witnessed. My father warned my mother not to let me contact any of you while Patrice was alive. Mamma thought it was to protect me, but I think he didn't want to embarrass his real family with me. Is that what this visit is about? Do you want to threaten me, too, if I go public?"

"I don't care who knows about you." Gio threw a hand up in the air. "If we're so embarrassed by you, why are we hosting a dinner for you tomorrow night?"

"I don't know." Gigi threw up both of her hands in a

similar frustrated gesture.

"Do you mind if I join you?" Julia asked softly from the doorway.

Gio waved his wife in. She went to his side and whispered something into his ear. He nodded and took a seat.

Julia then turned to Gigi and gave her a sympathetic smile. "Why don't we all sit down?"

In the face of Julia's sweet voice and calm nature, Gigi felt her anger draining out of her. She took the seat across from Gio. Julia sat beside her husband on the settee. She looked back and forth between them and said lightly, "Let's start over. Whenever I have a problem with someone I try to begin where we agree. Gio, you want to get to know your sister, don't you?"

"Why else would I have been trying to contact her for the last five years?" Gio asked gruffly. Julia gave him a look, and he shifted uncomfortably as if he were a child being reprimanded. Gigi would have found it amusing if her stomach wasn't tied up in so many nervous knots that she was afraid she'd lose her lunch on the expensive rug beneath her feet. Gio looked into his wife's eyes for a moment, then to Gigi's utter shock, his expression completely softened. "Yes, more than anything, I want Gigi here and in our lives."

Gigi's eyes were still round with surprise when Julia turned to her. "And Gigi, no matter what happened in the past, you're here because you want to get to know your brothers. Am I right?"

Gigi nodded and shrugged with one shoulder.

Julia took her husband's hand in hers. "Then that's

where you both start. That's what's important. Everything else will sort itself out if you remember why you're here." She met Gigi's eyes. "I'll let you in on a little secret about your brothers, Gigi. Something they can't tell you themselves. When you deal with them, it's best to pretend they were raised by wolves. Ignore the snarling and snapping. They don't mean it."

Gio arched an eyebrow at Julia and challenged, "Wolves?"

Julia looked back at him unapologetically. "Do you want my help or not?"

Gio inclined his head without another word, and Gigi marveled at the hint of humor in his eyes. "Go on."

Julia turned back to Gigi. "I heard some of what you said as I came in. Gio was wrong that day, but he was wrong for the right reason." She gave her husband's hand a supportive squeeze and quickly glanced up to check his expression. It was carefully blank. "I'm not saying anything we haven't spoken about, Gio. I know it would be nice to rewrite history or simply forget it, but there is still one person who deserves to hear it. She'll never be one of you until she does."

Gio took Julia's hand beneath his and placed it on his thigh as if he garnered some courage by doing so. "Father was right to hide you from my mother. For as long as I can remember, and until the day she died, she was consumed by an anger that knew no boundaries. She had no conscience. She would have turned you against us or destroyed you. I don't know what I would have done had I known about you the day I went to retrieve father's body. I'd like to think it would have changed everything, but who knows? My mother had a way of making the world look darker than it was." He shook his head. "No, it wasn't all her. I allowed myself to be manipulated. I followed where she led, but it was my choice to do so."

Julia leaned against Gio's side and said softly, "That's a harsher view than I take on what you did. You thought you were protecting your mother."

"I threatened to take the home away from Leora if she ever spoke of being with my father." He rubbed his hands over his face, and when he looked back at Gigi his eyes were full of a sadness Gigi understood too well. "I'll understand if you can't forgive me, Gigi, but don't let me be the reason you stay away from the rest of your family. You'll love Luke as a big brother. Although he may mother-hen you if you let him. He's flying back from Ohio tomorrow to meet you. I've never seen Nick as excited about anything as he was when he heard you were coming for a visit. And Max is flying in from visiting his in-laws in Florida to meet you. You don't have to stay with us if you don't want to, but don't leave. Not because of me."

Tears had started spilling down Gigi's cheeks as Gio spoke. He wasn't a man who seemed comfortable talking about his feelings or the past, but he was doing it for her, and it was both confusing and beautiful at the same time. It also made Gigi want to believe him more than she'd ever wanted anything in her life. "You really didn't know about me?"

"I didn't, Gigi. I swear it on my life."

Wiping away her tears, Gigi nodded. This was the man she'd witnessed once before, the brother she'd hoped he could be. "When I saw you with Julia at your wedding, you were different than how I remembered you."

Gio stood and said harshly, "You were at our wedding? How did no one know?"

Julia stood beside him and said, "Let me translate that for you. He means he wishes he had known because he would have loved to have shared our day with you."

Gigi met Julia's eyes and said with a touch of sarcasm, "Which you know because you speak wolf?"

"Fluently," Julia said, and a large smile spread across her face. "Lucky for you, it's not a difficult second language to acquire."

Gio shook his head in exasperation. "At work I'm a man people fear." He hugged Julia. "I don't suppose I can convince you to fear me just a little? You know, so the rest of the family doesn't turn on me like the wild pack they are."

Julia laughed and gave Gio a pat on the cheek. "I'm sorry to say, sweetie, but if we have a little girl there will be no saving you. She's going to wrap you around her little finger."

"Is that so?" He was smiling warmly, not at all afraid of the possibility. "And what if we have a boy?"

"I hope he turns out to be just as strong and as loyal as his father."

The scene should have been uncomfortable, but somehow Gigi didn't feel excluded. Watching her brother with his wife was actually reminding Gigi of a time in her childhood when her father had joked with her mother the same way.

For once, that memory wasn't accompanied by resentment. Could getting to know her brothers do more than reopen old wounds? Could it help heal them as well?

And how could she not admire Julia? She had walked into an escalating, explosive conversation and had somehow brought brother and sister to, if not a loving place, at least common ground. "You're going to be an amazing mother, Julia."

Julia blushed and hugged Gio. "I hope so. I've never been happier."

Gio wrapped both of his arms around her and kissed her forehead. "Me, either." He met Gigi's eyes over Julia's head. "We still have things we need to discuss, but they can wait. Tonight let's enjoy a quiet dinner. Tomorrow there won't be a peaceful place to hide in this house."

"Who's coming?" Gigi asked, suddenly a whole lot less sure what the next day would have in store for her.

Gio shrugged in resignation. "If I know my family, all of them."

Gigi's eyes flew to Julia's for confirmation that she might have misunderstood. Julia smiled back apologetically. "I've been fielding calls all day. Everyone wants to meet you, Gigi."

Gigi consoled herself with a thought she didn't share. *I guess that's better than no one wanting to.*

Julia pushed away from her husband and checked her watch. "I have to meet with our house staff if we're going to be ready for tomorrow. I was planning on fifty, Gio. You said Luke and Max are flying in. Are others doing the same?"

"Probably," Gio said with a groan.

Julia spoke as she absently gave Gigi a hug. "I'll plan for a hundred, then, but I'll have extra food prepared just in case more come."

"A hundred?" Gigi sat down with a thud.

Julia chuckled. "Welcome to the family, Gigi."

✧   ✧   ✧

KANE ROLLED OVER in his bed and pulled a blanket over his head to stop the sunlight from searing through his still-closed eyelids. He hadn't imbibed that much Scotch since his college days, and his thirty-five-year-old body was making him pay for every sip of it. His head was throbbing. His stomach was churning. If death didn't feel like this, it was close.

"I told the office you had a stomach bug," his father said from a chair beside Kane's bed. Only Thom Sander would call in Kane's absence as if his son was home sick from school and not the CEO of one of the country's most profitable companies.

"I have a nine a.m. meeting I can't cancel on." The sound of his own voice was like a sledgehammer to his temple.

"Then it's a shame it's noon," his father said dryly.

Kane sat straight up, almost lost the contents of his stomach on himself, then lay back down and covered his face with one arm. "Fuck. Ritmon does not like to be canceled on."

"He'll survive. He wants the deal as much as you do."

"And you know that because?"

"I have my sources."

"Dad, you're retired. You're not supposed to call my office and pump my people for information. And they know better than to tell you anything."

"I hired half of them. And you should be grateful. Just because you run the company now, doesn't mean I'm too senile to give you pointers now and then."

Kane rolled onto his side and calculated the possibility of things getting very messy if he moved again. "I can't argue about this right now. Thank you for calling the office. I'll call them myself in about an hour."

"You should have had the water and aspirin I tried to give you last night, but you were convinced you weren't drunk."

Kane groaned again. "I don't remember that."

"I'm not surprised. Your mother wanted to come over. She has her grandmother's hangover cocktail. You can thank me later for saving you from that."

"She knows I was drinking?"

"I wasn't going to lie to her. I had to tell her why I wasn't coming home last night."

"You didn't have to stay, Dad. I'm not a kid anymore."

"You'll understand when you have a family of your own, Kane. So, what are you going to do about Gigi?"

"Gigi?" Kane opened one eye.

His father crossed one leg over the other and looked at Kane with a wry smile. "Don't even try to act like you don't know what I'm talking about. You spilled the whole story to me last night. Twice. You started to tell me a third time, but thankfully passed out before you could."

Kane closed his eyes. "That's just fucking perfect."

"I'd tell you to mind your language, but I'll hold off until I'm sure you're completely sober. Then I'll toss in a lecture about how alcohol never makes anything better and get it all done at once."

"Funny, Dad. I'd laugh, but I'm not up to it right this moment."

"Sarcasm, that's a good sign. Sounds like you're going to live."

"That is yet to be determined."

"Not that you asked for my opinion, but it looks like you and Gio need to talk."

"Dad, I'm willing to pay you a million dollars if you go home now."

His father laughed. "Most of your money is still my money until I die, so please, as a rule, offer smaller bribes."

Kane opened his bloodshot eyes again. "Is this payback for something I did to you as a child? Because I don't remember giving you shit like this."

His father looked on with amusement he made no attempt to hide. "Kane, if you could see yourself right now, you'd be laughing, too. If I find you like this again, I'll start to worry, but for now, I'm just enjoying watching the almighty Kane trying not to throw up all over himself. You were born thinking you'd rule the world, but a bottle of Scotch nearly did you in. Humbling, isn't it? How frail we all are at the end of the day."

"Dad, if you don't stop talking I'm going to kick your ass." He moved his head and made a pained sound. "Or I will as soon as the room stops spinning."

He father walked out of the room and returned with a glass of water and a pill. "Drink this, and go back to sleep if you can. You'll feel better when you wake up."

Kane obediently swallowed the pill and the water then dropped back onto the bed. "I'm an idiot."

His father sat back down on the chair near Kane's bed. "No more than most people, but I do want to make sure you handle this thing with Gigi the right way. You and Gio have been friends a long time. I'd hate to see that end over something like this."

Kane closed his eyes again. "There is no this. I don't have to tell Gio anything because nothing happened. Nothing is going to happen. I don't know what I said last night, but it was the Scotch talking, not me. Maybe I find Gigi attractive, but the world is full of beautiful women. My phone is full of numbers of gorgeous women who would be here in five minutes if I asked them to. I don't have the time or the desire to get into anything as complicated as *doing* anything with Gigi would be. Frankly, she's not worth the trouble."

His father gave him a pat on the shoulder and picked up the empty glass from the nightstand. "Okay, but call me if you need to talk about it. I wasn't always this old, you know. I remember what it was like when I first saw your mother. I was stupid in love with her. Still am. I'm glad she wasn't my best friend's little sister because I couldn't have walked away from her for anyone or anything." He walked over and closed the drapes, bringing blissful darkness once again to Kane. "Get some sleep, Kane. Don't worry about the office. I'll head over there now and make sure everything is going smoothly."

Kane went to sit up again then stopped himself. "Dad?"

"Yes?"

"Thanks. Tell Marge I'll be there in a couple of hours."

"Get some rest, Kane. You want to look human for Gio's dinner tonight."

"If I spilled everything to you last night, then I'm sure I told you I'm not going."

His father gave him a look he knew well. Without words it said, "I expect better from you." So far, it had never failed to sway Kane. His father was a good man who wanted the best for his children. It was hard to look him in the eye and not want to be deserving of that kind of parent.

"Dad, it's not wise for me to see Gigi again."

The look persisted. "Gio has been like a brother to you, like a son to me. I'll be there at the dinner, and so will you. And if it's too damn hard to look at his sister, then you wait until you can speak to Gio alone, and you tell him the truth. But don't let it keep you away from what is a very important dinner for your best friend. My son doesn't hide from problems. He faces them head on. It's the only way to win."

"There is no winner or loser in this. Trust me, Gio would prefer I stay away from his sister."

Shaking his head, he said, "I'd agree with you if I thought there was a chance in hell that was going to happen." He paused at the door. "And watch your language. I raised you better than that."

Kane lay in his bed in his Upper West Side apartment staring up at the dark ceiling. Getting involved in each other's lives, regardless of whether or not they were asked to, was practically a family pastime. On a good day, it was one of the things Kane loved most about his family. There weren't many Sanders, but they were fiercely protective of each other. It wasn't surprising his father had stayed at his bedside the whole night.

Mortifying that at thirty-five Kane had given his father reason to, but Kane didn't resent his intrusion. The older he got, the more he admired his father and the way he handled himself.

I just hope he's wrong this time.
I can't have feelings for Gigi. Gio would never forgive me.

Never before had he been faced with a temptation he didn't know if he could resist. There had to be something he could do to take his mind off how much he wanted Gigi. Kane rolled over and dialed the first number on his phone. As soon as he heard someone pick up, he said, "Lynn, it's Kane. Would you like to attend a party with me tonight?"

Chapter Nine

GIGI STEPPED AWAY from the crowd of people who had spilled into every downstairs room of her brother's home and slipped into what she hoped was the sanctuary of the kitchen. Her face was sore from smiling, and she'd thought she was a person who enjoyed hugs, but now she realized everything was better in moderation. In the beginning she'd tried to remember the names of everyone who rushed over and threw their arms around her as if they weren't complete strangers to her. It was odd to be in a house full of people who wanted to meet her and still feel so alone.

Instead of the quiet she'd sought, the kitchen was a flurry of cooks and staff, rushing to fill plates. A man with a thick French accent was barking orders while the man beside him grew more sweaty and nervous. He picked a shrimp spring roll off a tray and held it up. "Look at this. I wouldn't serve this to my dog. When did you prepare these? Yesterday? Last week? I hope sometime this year, yes? You cannot serve this. Start over."

The man beside him waved a hand frantically around him. "Start over? There is no time. We'll have to make do with what we have."

The Frenchman began to swear in French. "You're fired. Get out of this kitchen."

"Sir, I'm sorry, but you're not the one who hired me."

The Frenchman walked toward him while shedding his dinner coat. "But I am the one who will throw you out the door with my bare hands. Your choice, walk or fly." He picked up the tray of appetizers and dumped the contents into the trash. "I could not sleep tonight if I let this pass as food."

Standing at the door of the kitchen, the man held up his phone. "I don't know what to do. If I call my brother and tell him I messed up the first gig he put me in charge of, he'll never trust me with one again. Should I leave? Do I take my staff with me? You . . . or someone . . . signed a contract. You'll still have to pay for today. I don't have the money to pay my brother for all these supplies if you don't. I'm sorry they aren't perfect. I don't know what they're supposed to look like. All I know is I need this job, and if I leave I can kiss it goodbye, brother or no brother."

After saying something harshly in his language, the Frenchman seemed to calm. He rolled his eyes skyward then clapped his hands. A hush fell over the kitchen. "If you work here normally, raise your hand. Everyone else, step to the left of that table." With the regular house chef at his side, they organized the staff and soon the kitchen was running smoothly, and the Frenchman seemed satisfied. He waved for the man at the door to return and held up a batch of shrimp spring rolls. "This is what a fresh spring roll looks like." He tossed it to the man. "Taste it. Good food, like a good woman, is always worth the wait. Now, organize your people to serve this as it comes out. No one needs to know about this, but have some pride in what you serve. Especially if you represent your brother."

The Frenchman rolled his sleeves back down and picked up his jacket. He caught Gigi watching him, and his face transformed as he smiled. "Gigi, do you cook?"

Gigi glanced around awkwardly at the staff, who were curiously watching her. Perhaps she would have learned had she stayed with her mother in Venice. She could easily imagine her mother being just as opinionated about every item that came out of her kitchen. "No, not like this."

"You forgot me already?" He walked toward her, not at all the intimidating man he'd been a few moments before. "I'm Richard, Maddy's husband. Don't worry; I know you met half of New York today. It's a bit overwhelming at first, non?"

"Yes," Gigi said with a relieved sigh. "I remember Maddy said you were a chef."

"Yes. Yes, I am. Don't tell Maddy what you saw in here. She told me not to come into the kitchen, but I couldn't help myself. Why should what we put in our mouths be less perfect than what we hang on our walls? Because it is more fleeting? Life is fleeting, but—" He stopped at the look on Gigi's face. "Sorry. I am passionate about food."

Gigi let out a breathy laugh. "Apparently."

He studied her face again. "Are you hungry or hiding?"

"Regrouping," Gigi said with a self-deprecating smile.

Richard pulled a stool away from a counter and motioned for her to sit on it. He took the one across from her. "A family the size of yours is not easy to get to know, but they are good people."

"They seem to be."

"This was the first time you met your brothers, yes?"

"Yes. And they seem wonderful, too. Their wives are also nice."

Richard poured each of them a glass of wine. "Yet you look sad."

Gigi accepted the drink. She suddenly wished she'd brought her mother with her. How strange that it took going so far away from her to want to be with her. "I was afraid it would be awful here, but I also hoped it would be different . . ."

"Have you had a chance to talk to your brothers yet?"

Gigi found it surprisingly easy to open up to Richard. She had a feeling he didn't do or say much if he didn't want to. If he was asking her questions, he was interested in the answers, simple as that. "Only briefly, except Gio. I'm staying here with Julia and him."

Richard nodded. "After tonight, you'll have time with your brothers. Think of this as an initiation by fire."

Gigi chuckled. "Or death by excessive hugging."

Richard laughed along with her. "Yes, but there are worse ways to die." He stood up. "Come, you can't spend the evening in here. Nor can I, even if I would like to. If I must suffer the groping, then so must you."

They walked into the hallway together, still smiling. Gigi

came to an abrupt halt, however, when she spotted someone she'd been trying not to think about since he'd left her the day before. There he was, just as gorgeous as she remembered. He looked perfectly at home at the party as well as in his expensive suit. A tall blonde woman, who Gigi cattily thought resembled a plastic Barbie, hung on his arm like a decoration. Each time he spoke, she laughed and rubbed herself against him. Gigi tried, but she couldn't look away.

As if sensing her, Kane raised his eyes to her. Gigi's breath caught in her throat, and she took a step back. She didn't want to feel the heat that always swept through her beneath his gaze. She cursed herself for wanting a man who was clearly not interested in her. For reading what she wanted into the way he looked at her. Because for just a moment she'd almost convinced herself he wanted nothing more than to walk away from the woman he'd brought and come to her side. Kane had brought a date to her welcome home party. If she was still wondering if he was interested in her, he couldn't have been clearer.

He turned away, and Gigi gasped from the physical pain she felt at his rejection.

Richard studied her expression and shook his head. "Oh, Gigi, there is nothing there for you but trouble."

Gigi straightened and started walking. "Where?" she asked, as if she had no idea what he was referring to.

"L'amour fait les plus grandes douceurs et les plus sensibles infortunes de la vie," Richard said as he walked beside her. Gigi understood enough to get the gist of what he was saying, but she pretended not to. Richard added, "It's a very old quote: Love makes life's sweetest pleasures and worst misfortunes." Richard glanced over at Kane, who was still standing with the overly affectionate blonde. "Be careful, Gigi."

Gigi followed his gaze, then gave herself an inner smack. She refused to spend another moment mooning over a man who couldn't have been more obvious about how he felt about her. Gigi excused herself from Richard. "It was really nice speaking with you, Richard. But you're right; I should go hunt down my brothers. They're the reason I'm here."

✧ ✧ ✧

"How long do we have to pretend to care about who just had which baby? I'd rather be asking, my place or yours?" Lynn Thistle whispered into Kane's ear.

"What did you say?" Kane asked absently, keeping his eyes focused on a plant on the far side of the room because he refused to turn to see if Gigi was still in the room.

"Earth to Kane. You asked me out not the other way around. The least you can do is pretend to be listening to me."

Kane nodded without looking at Lynn. Bringing her had been a mistake. He'd had fun with her in the past. They were friends of sorts. Sometimes more than friends, but never anything serious. "Sorry, I'm horrendously hung over."

She knew him too well to accept that. "No, that's not it. Are you sleeping with someone's wife?"

Kane's attention snapped to Lynn. "Why would you ask that?"

She tapped him on the chest. "Because you couldn't care less that I'm with you. I'd be offended if it weren't sort of sweet. You have that guilty lover look about you. Is it someone who won't leave her husband for you? Or someone you'd like to make jealous? If so, I bet she's dying, watching you here with me."

Kane shook his head in indulgent amusement at her antics. "Is that why you're hanging all over me? You're evil."

Her perfectly shaped eyebrows rose. "Me? I'm not the one who wasn't honest about what he wanted tonight. We've known each other a long time, Kane. You could have simply asked me for my help."

Kane smiled at how unflappable Lynn was. She had a practical, hold-nothing-back attitude he admired. If he could choose who to have feelings for, Lynn would have made sense for him. Yes, she was a tad more flamboyant than his usual taste, but she was easy to get along with. She deserved better than how he was treating her. "Do you want to leave?"

Lynn shrugged. "Only if you do. It is not every day I am in a room with so many gorgeous, rich men. Do you know which ones are single?"

Kane cocked his head to the side. "Won't it be hard to hook up with someone when you're obviously with me?"

Lynn clung to his arm as if he'd just said the sexiest, most romantic thing. "Honey, how can you be a man and not understand how they think? You are a serious hunk. Half the men here are asking themselves if they could win me away from you. We just have to find the right one and then let him think he did."

Lynn was most probably right. At five foot seven—ten if you count the sexy heels she had on—blonde, blue-eyed and gorgeous, Lynn was most men's wet dream. Her blue, skintight dress left little of her curves to a man's imagination. It was a shame he didn't want to sample her again. But she was right. He wasn't interested. *How could I be, with Gigi in the room?*

He threw his head back and laughed, both at himself and at Lynn's joke. "You win. Pick someone, and I'll tell you what I know about him."

Lynn threw her arms around his neck and quickly kissed him full on the lips in gratitude. "I'll invite you to the wedding."

Wedding.

The mere mention of one reminded him of Gigi and the heat of their first encounter. Why did she have to be someone he wouldn't allow himself to have?

Kane looked over Lynn's head and scanned the room. Off in one corner, Gigi was talking to Luke and Max but paused as if feeling his attention. Her eyes met his. He wanted to pull Lynn's arms down from around his neck, but he didn't.

It was better for Gigi to think he was with someone.

He lowered his head and kissed Lynn back.

Lynn gave him a funny look. "I thought you weren't . . . oh, is she watching us? Then let's give her something worth seeing." She pulled his head down and kissed him fully.

It wasn't the passionate kiss he'd shared with Gigi, but it wasn't a hardship either. He tried to lose himself in it, told himself good could be good enough.

But it wasn't.

It left him feeling worse instead of better.

He raised his head and looked for Gigi, but she was gone. He stepped back from Lynn.

"So?" Lynn asked. "Did it work?"

Kane nodded sadly. "Yes, it did." *Because I'm an asshole. Gigi's better off without me.*

Chapter Ten

"You would think the prank would have gotten old, but Max got so angry every time we did it, we couldn't help ourselves, we had to do it again." Nick Andrade sipped on a clear soda as he lounged on the couch in Gio's library.

His wife, Rena, had shed her shoes and was curled up against his side. "It stopped when I came into the picture, but probably not before Max had enough memories of torture to tell a therapist."

Nick kissed Rena on the cheek. "Killjoy. You were bossy even in your teens."

Rena gave his leg a pat. "I can't imagine what the housekeeper thought of all of those frogs showing up in the house."

✧ ✧ ✧

Max shuddered from his standing position near the fire. "Can we talk about something more pleasant? Just the thought of frogs makes me squeamish."

His wife, Tara, laughed up at him and swung his hand in

hers. "Is it wrong that I love that about you? You're always so independent and sure of yourself. I ask myself why you need me. Then I remember your fear of frogs . . ." She went up on her tiptoes to kiss him on the lips briefly. "I want you to know I'll always be there to protect you from those vicious amphibians."

Gio added, "Max, you can hide behind your wife and Rena only so much. Eventually you'll leave your shoes unattended when they're not around to defend them. It may be Nick, me, or perhaps one of our offspring perpetuating the tradition, but there is no escaping it."

Julia raised her hand to cover her smile. Gigi chuckled. How could she not? Individually her brothers were nicer than she'd ever imagined, but together they were hilarious.

In mock irritation, Max wagged a finger of reprimand at each person in the room. "You're all assholes." He looked across at Gigi. "I expect this from them, but you, too, Gigi?"

Gigi smiled and shrugged, feeling lighthearted for the first time since she'd arrived.

Nick brought a hand jokingly to his chest. "That hurts, Max. It's true, but it cuts deeply."

Julia winked at Gigi. "This is them getting along."

Rena leaned forward and tapped the table in front of her. "No joke. I used to worry about these boys. I can't tell you how nice it is to see them like this."

Luke looked completely comfortable lounging on the arm of the leather couch with his wife, Cassie, seated on one of his thighs. "Rena, I can't imagine what our family would have done without you. You and your parents gave us a second home when we most needed one."

Cassie smiled at Rena. "I love Thom and Helen. They're sitcom perfect parents. Funny, but kind of Middle America wholesome. I bet they never let Kane torment you."

Rena pointed at Gio. "Are you kidding me? Gio and Kane made it impossible for me to date all through high school. The first boy I brought home? They hung him over the banister of the porch until he cried. Cried. You try to date after that. I thought we were in for round two of that when they found out I was dating Nick." She hugged Nick. "It got dicey there for a while, but it worked out. Gigi, I feel for you and whatever man you bring home to this crew. Talk about over-protective."

From beside Gio, Julia asked, "Do you have a special someone in your life?"

Irrationally, stupidly, an image of Kane danced in Gigi's thoughts, and because of it she answered angrily, "No, no one." The mood of the room temporarily sobered, and Gigi felt awkward for not making light of the question. "It doesn't matter. I'm perfectly happy alone. Normally my business takes up most of my time anyway. You know how it is when you work for yourself, there is no tougher boss."

Tara interjected happily, "I'm sure all that will change now." All eyes turned to Tara, and the room became tensely quiet. Tara's cheeks went bright pink. "So, we haven't told her yet?"

Gigi's stomach tightened nervously.

Gio straightened to his full height. "She was tired last night, and today didn't seem appropriate."

Gigi searched each of her brother's faces quickly. "What is it?"

Luke shifted Cassie off his lap and went to stand beside Gigi. He raised a hand to stop Gio from speaking. "We didn't know how to tell you. Gio will try to shoulder the blame for it, but none of us knew what to do. We tried to contact you personally. We reached out via lawyers. You refused to communicate with us at all. Leora said our attempts were upsetting you and asked us to wait for you to come to us. So, that's what we did. And here you are. I can see why Gio would put off saying anything that could cause you to pull away from us again."

Gigi searched the room again for a clue of what they were talking about. "Okay, now you're scaring me."

Nick stood and went to stand beside Luke. "It's actually good news."

Max joined his brothers. "Although I would have wanted to know earlier. Even if I wasn't talking to us."

Gio moved closer. "It doesn't change anything, though, Gigi. Remember that."

Standing, hands clasped nervously in front of her, Gigi faced all four of her brothers as her mind flew to the worst possible announcement. *Am I'm not actually related to them? Did they bring me here to tell me that?* Her stomach churned, her hands went cold. "Just fucking say it."

Gio's eyebrows rose at her choice of language, but he answered calmly, "Our father had a will that was hidden until a few years ago. It divided our father's estate evenly between the five of us. Your portion has been put aside in a trust fund for you, Gigi. Although you haven't had access to it, nor have we, it's been accumulating interest for you and is substantial enough there is no reason for you to work another day in your life unless you choose to. It will easily support you and your mother if that's what you choose to do with it. Or we can help you invest a portion of it in stocks, and you can live off the dividends."

Gigi swayed as she digested the news. It was too much to take in, especially with all of them watching her reaction. "How much money are we talking about?"

"We liquefied the assets before dividing them. Your trust fund was originally just under a billion."

"A billion? As in one billion US dollars?" Gigi asked, trying to wrap her mind around what that would mean to her and her mother. What it would have meant had it been given to her at her father's passing. Would her life have been better or worse? Gio had said that his mother would have tried to destroy her. Had not knowing about it kept her safer? Her brothers said they would have told her about the will if she had met with them. She wanted to believe them.

Nick shrugged in almost an apology. "We did have to split it five ways. But, we can show you how to double that amount through investments."

Julia walked over and put a steadying arm around Gigi's waist. "I don't think she's worried that it's not enough." She led Gigi over to one of the couches and sat down beside her. "Are you okay, Gigi? I know it's a lot to take in."

Gigi rubbed her temples with both hands. "How long have you all known about this?"

Max went to sit across from her. "Tara and I found the will in the back of my mother's journal before she died. A little over three years ago. Do you remember when I flew out to meet you in London? I wanted to tell you then."

Gio stepped closer and said gruffly, "I sent a lawyer to speak with you, but you refused to meet with him, too."

"I was still angry," Gigi whispered. It all sounded too perfect. Too good to be true. "So, what's the catch? What do I have to do to get it?"

Luke sat down on her other side. "Nothing, Gigi. It's yours. For now, Gio is the trustee of the fund. But only because coming into that kind of money overnight can be overwhelming. And confusing. It's not like it's all in one bank account. That kind of money needs to be protected."

"I don't understand. Is it mine or not mine?"

Max interjected. "We decided to give it to you in a controlled manner. That's why Gio has management of it for now. Although it sounds like an insane amount of money, we don't want you to lose it because you came into it too quickly and didn't have time to adapt. Your life won't be the same after today."

Gigi shook her head in confusion. "You make my inheritance sound like a bad thing."

Luke added, "Money changes things, Gigi. It changes you and the people around you. You won't know who your real friends are anymore. People will like you because of what you have, or what you can do for them. In some ways having money is freeing, in others it can isolate you. We can help you through all that."

Gio said, "You'll need security, especially if word of your inheritance gets out. So, for now, I wouldn't tell anyone."

Nick joked, "You'll need the names of the best rehab facilities, because suddenly you can afford all the good drugs."

Gio glared at Nick. "She's not doing drugs."

Nick shrugged. "I'm trying to be practical here. People lose their minds when they come into money. That's what all of my friends did when they finally got their trust funds."

Max sighed. "Rena, you need to choose Nick's friends from now on. He obviously has awful taste."

Gio cut in. "Gigi is not going to do drugs. She's not going to go on a crazy spending spree. She's twenty-five years old and a businesswoman. I have faith in her."

Julia gave her husband a proud smile.

Gigi bristled despite his kind words. She stood and felt a little dizzy. "I'm trying to take this all in, and you're right, it's overwhelming. I can't process it while you're looking at me, talking like I'm not here. I think I'm going to be sick. Excuse me."

She rushed toward the door.

Luke stood as if to follow her, but Gio stopped him. "Let her go. She needs a minute."

Luke nodded. "I hope we handled this right."

Max went to stand beside him. "That was not at all how I imagined it. I pictured her much happier."

Nick gave Gio a comforting pat on the back. "She's upset, but she'll come around. Most likely better than any of us would because she doesn't have our mother in her."

Rena slid beneath Nick's arm and elbowed him in the

side. "I want to tell you how wrong that was to say, but you're probably right."

✧ ✧ ✧

FRESH FROM CAUTIOUSLY handing off a happy Lynn to a newly divorced Andrade cousin from Connecticut, who was smiling like he'd pulled off the coup of the century, Kane was in the foyer debating if he should stay or head home. Part of him felt he should stick around long enough to make sure Lynn's choice wasn't a weasel, but he knew nothing nefarious would go down while the patriarchs of the family were in attendance. Even though they appeared easygoing, Alessandro and Victor were the heart and the fist of the family.

The door of Gio's library opened. Gigi flew out of it and rushed out the front door of the house. She looked pale and upset. If he had thought that bringing Lynn would upset her that much, he wouldn't have.

If I had thought it out at all, I wouldn't have.

That's my problem. I can't think straight when I'm around her.

Kane didn't hesitate for a second. He was at the front entrance in a heartbeat. Somehow he had to make this right. "Gigi."

Gigi swung around, her eyes flashing with anger. "Shouldn't you be with your date?"

Kane grabbed one of Gigi's arms. "Lynn and I aren't serious. I thought if I brought her—"

Gigi pulled her arm free and hissed, "I don't care about

you. Or your blonde Barbie. I get it; you're not attracted to me. Can we not go over this again right now? I came out here to clear my head."

She walked a few feet away from Kane. He followed her. *Maybe she's not upset about me.* The thought made him feel better and worse all at the same time. "What happened?"

She looked out over the darkened lawn while holding onto a pillar for support. "Too much to put into words easily. I don't know what to think. How I feel. Even if my brothers are telling me the truth, nothing will ever be the same. Can my whole life change just like that? What if I don't want it to?"

Kane guessed what she was referring to. "They told you about your inheritance."

Gigi swung around to face him. "You knew?"

"I spoke to Gio yesterday. It bothered me that your father had left you nothing."

Gigi turned away from him again. "Apparently he left me one fifth of his estate. I don't know if I want it. Who wouldn't, though? I have to be crazy to even think that, don't I?"

"Gigi," Kane said softly. Her obvious distress made him want to pull her into his arms. The mere thought of holding her brought a rush of pent-up desire raging to the surface. She was a hunger no one else could appease. "I don't want to confuse you more—"

Without turning to look at him, Gigi said just as softly, "Don't worry, Kane, I get that you're not interested in me. Just because I feel something doesn't mean you—"

He swung her around and took her beautiful face in his hands. Her eyes, so innocently yearning, sent him over the edge. He couldn't help himself. He had to taste her. His lips brushed over hers gently, and she came alive beneath his touch.

He dug his hands into her hair, plunging his tongue between her sweet lips. She opened herself wider for him, grabbing at his shirt as if she needed it to steady herself. Two tongues, hotly exploring each other. It shouldn't have had the power to send Kane over the edge, but it did. There was no right. No wrong. Just this mutual need that demanded to be appeased.

In his mind, he had already hiked up her skirt and was fucking her against the porch banister. He didn't care who saw them or what they thought. He wanted to claim her as his and pound into her until she cried out his name in climax.

Her hands were everywhere on him, sweetly exploring his back, his ass. He tightened his hands in her hair, fearing that if he let himself the fantasy in his head would become a scandalous reality.

"It's a beautiful night out here, isn't it?" Thom asked after clearing his throat loudly.

Kane broke off the kiss and turned to face his father. He moved to hide Gigi behind him. He could only imagine how he looked. His breathing was ragged, and he felt wild in a way he'd never experienced before. "Dad . . . could you give us a minute?"

Thom shook his head slowly. "We need to talk, Kane."

Gigi eased out from behind Kane. Her cheeks were bright pink. "I should return to the party." With that she bolted back into the house.

Alone again, Kane took several deep breaths before saying, "Dad, it's not how it looked."

His father went to stand beside him and leaned back against the banister. "Thank God, because earlier you were kissing a woman in full view of everyone at the party, and now you're outside making moves on Gigi. None of that is what I'd call acceptable behavior. But enlighten me. Which part of this is *not* the way it looks?"

Kane groaned. His excitement dissolved quickly beneath the anger he saw in his father's eyes. Guilt washed over him. There was no excuse for what he'd done that night, but he attempted an explanation. "I invited Lynn so nothing would happen between Gigi and me."

"Does Lynn know that?"

"She does now," Kane admitted reluctantly. If the expression on his father's face was anything to go by, his honesty hadn't redeemed him at all.

"Is that why she's hanging all over Kyle Barrington in the solarium?"

"Yes," Kane said, feeling a bit guilty about even that. Before Gigi he would have said he was above anything even resembling the idiocy he was presently perpetuating. He was a grown man. A successful CEO. What was it about Gigi that reduced him to feeling like a guilty juvenile?

"And Gigi?" Thom asked, still clearly not pleased with his son.

"I don't know, Dad. I don't fucking know what I'm doing."

Thom put a supportive hand on Kane's shoulder and sighed. "That much, son, is painfully clear."

Chapter Eleven

G IGI DUCKED INTO the first door off the hallway and found herself surrounded by racks and racks of coats. She didn't care where she was as long as it gave her a moment away from everyone.

Kane kissed me.

And, God, it was good.

Her hand went to her lips. Her whole body was still humming from Kane's touch. How could one man have the power to bring her so much pleasure? His tongue had only briefly danced with hers, but remembering his taste, the feel of him inside her, left her craving more of him with an intensity that scared her.

She closed her eyes and savored the sensations rushing through her. Her sex was throbbing and unrepentantly wet. She was tempted to slide her hand down the front of her skirt and stroke herself while imagining what they would have done next had they not been interrupted. She didn't touch herself, but she wanted to. Oh, how she wanted to.

The door of the coat closet opened, and Gigi spun around to see Julia step inside and close the door discreetly behind her. "Are you okay, Gigi? I saw you come in here and not come back out. I was worried."

Gigi let out a long shudder of breath. *You almost saw much worse than that.* Gigi wondered what her sweet sister-in-law would have said had she caught her masturbating with the coats. The image was so embarrassing and ridiculous that Gigi started laughing and couldn't stop. As she did, Julia started to look concerned, which only made Gigi laugh more. She laughed until she started to cry. Once she started to cry, all of the emotions within her poured out through the long-suppressed tears. There were tears of happiness, sadness, fear, letting go, confusion, and frustration all wrapped together in big weepy tangle that had found its release.

Julia stepped closer and put an arm around Gigi. "We probably shouldn't have invited everyone to meet you all at once. Was it too much?"

Gigi pulled herself together with a loud sniff. "No, the party was wonderful. I love that the whole family came to see me." Her bottom lip quivered and fresh tears threatened. "It's exactly the way I always dreamed it would be."

Julia patted her back softly. "Okay, so some of these tears are happy ones, right?"

Gigi nodded. She wiped her cheek with the back of one hand. "I am not the emotional basket case I presently appear to be. I can't remember the last time I cried. It's just so . . ." She stopped and tried to gather her thoughts. "Before I came here, I thought my brothers were the problem. But look at me. They've been nothing but nice to me, and I can't stop freaking out. Hell, they just told me I have an inheritance, and I'm hiding in a coat closet. Shouldn't I be toasting with champagne or calling my mother to fly her over to celebrate? Instead, I'm scared. I don't know what to do or how to feel. What is wrong with me?"

Julia continued to massage Gigi's back gently. "There's nothing wrong with you. When amazing things happen, we wonder if they're real and if they can last, because experience has taught us that often they're not, and they don't. But this is real, Gigi, and your brothers love you. Everything else is just icing on the cake. Yes, you now have money, but if you lost it tomorrow the important parts of all this wouldn't change. You'd still be a beautiful, independent woman with a wonderful mother and a slew of family who adore you simply because you're one of them. You're also lucky enough to be staying in a house with more than one large closet if you decide you need to hide again."

Gigi chuckled even though she still felt more than a little ridiculous. "Since you're so good with advice, what would you say if I told you I like Kane?"

Julia made a soft click as she chose her next words. "That's a tricky one. Gio wouldn't handle that well, but he's your brother, not your keeper. You have every right to be with whoever you want to be with. On the other hand, Kane brought a woman with him tonight who he seems to like . . . a lot, if appearances are anything to go by. I'd be careful."

Having no one else to confide in, Gigi admitted, "Kane kissed me. Just before I ran in here."

Julia pursed her lips. "Oh, boy."

Gigi leaned back against the coat rack and closed her

eyes. "I'm usually pretty levelheaded, but I feel out of control right now. With Kane. With everything my brothers just told me. I don't know if I'm hopeful or terrified, turned on or just flat-out confused that he kissed me."

Julia was quiet for a moment. "I don't know what to tell you about Kane. He has been a good friend to Gio for a long time, and I adore him, but I've never seen him date anyone for long. If you really want my advice, you should wait until your life settles down some."

Julia was a calming voice of reason. Gigi hugged her tightly. "Thank you."

Julia smiled warmly. "You're going to be fine; you know that, don't you? Now, let's get back to the party."

Gigi squared her shoulders and walked over to the door, placing her hand on the doorknob. "Don't tell anyone what I said about Kane, okay?"

Julia nodded once then raised a hand as a thought came to her. "I won't, but do yourself a favor, and don't tell your cousin Maddy. I won't say more than that. Just trust me on this one."

✧ ✧ ✧

KANE PAUSED IN the middle of typing an email to watch a plane draw a white line in the sky. Although he tried not to, he wondered if Gigi was still in flight or already back in Scotland. He told himself that her leaving was a good thing. Life could finally get back to normal.

It had been a month since he'd attended Gigi's welcome-home dinner. Twenty-nine days of avoiding her and anything that might remind him of her. Which was impossible since everything did. Other women no longer appealed to him. People in general annoyed him. Food tasted like cardboard. He was miserable.

He told himself he'd get over it. That one day he'd look back and be relieved that he'd made the right choice—for both of them.

For everyone.

He pushed away the sandwich his secretary, Marge, had ordered for him. She accused him of burning his candle at both ends. She wasn't far off. He'd taken his pent-up frustration and used it productively, aggressively. For the past month, he'd lengthened his normally long workday, often to include international conferences at all hours of the night. He'd hit the office gym just as hard. He wasn't sleeping much, but he didn't care. He was determined to stay focused. With that thought, he forced himself to finish his emails.

When he looked up an hour later, Marge was at the door of the office with her purse on her arm saying she'd see him the next day.

"Are you staying here tonight?"

"Depends," Kane answered, stretching in his office chair. "I may have an early morning London conference call. I'm seeing a real change over there since I've started conference calling with them personally."

"No doubt," Marge said. "I hear you lit a fire under that team. But you do need to sleep, Kane. Should I order a bed for your office?"

Her sarcasm was not missed. Kane gave her a lopsided, tired smile. "The couch is fine."

Marge shook her head and made a tsk-tsk sound. "I was joking." When Kane didn't say anything in response, Marge added, "I'll have a dry-cleaned suit delivered tomorrow morning." It wasn't the first time Kane had worked through the night, but Marge knew this was different.

After she left, Kane leaned back in his chair and stared at the ceiling above his desk. His father had always said: Acknowledge the problem. Face it head on.

Kane's present problem was he wanted a woman he shouldn't have. His solution was to pour himself into productive pursuits. By some standards, it was working. He hadn't seen Gigi, work projects were coming in ahead of schedule, and there was a possibility of a European expansion if sales continued to increase abroad.

He stood, and a muscle in his side clenched in protest at being motionless for so many hours. He headed into the washroom attached to his office and changed into workout clothing. Several sets of weights and a good run on the treadmill would clear his head.

One month. It had never taken that long to forget the taste of a woman, the scent of her, the feel of her lips beneath his. Kane threw a towel across the back of his neck and headed out of his office. Regardless of how he felt about Gigi, he'd made his decision. If it took six months, a year, two years, of working around the clock to end his fixation with her, that's what he would do.

It wasn't just about how Gio might feel about Kane dating his little sister; it was also the look Kane had seen in Gigi's eyes each time she'd talked about her family. She'd spent a lifetime yearning for what was becoming a reality for her—a relationship with her brothers. He refused to jeopardize that in any way.

She deserved this time with her family.

But, damn, I want her.

Chapter Twelve

GIGI WALKED INTO her West End Edinburgh office with Annelise's favorite skinny latte and a thick manila folder.

Annelise brushed her wild, blonde hair out of her face and smiled. "You're back." She rushed from behind her desk to hug her. "And you brought lattes. I love you! How was it?"

Gigi placed the folder on a small table and sat down facing Annelise on the leather couch that had taken six months for the two of them to be able to afford. "It was crazy, but good. I'm sorry I didn't call. A month sounded like a long time when I originally planned it, but it went by too quickly. I looked up, and it was time to come home."

Annelise hugged her again. "I'm glad you said home. I'll admit when you originally said you'd be staying there for so long I started to worry. One taste of the sweet life and you might not want to come back."

"The sweet life?"

"You said your brothers have money. The way I saw it, there were only two ways that could go. Either you'd feel out of place, or you'd fit right in. If you loved it there, I imagined they'd offer to take you in and let you stay and, really, who could blame you if you did?" Annelise picked up her coffee and took a sip of it. "Outside of me. I'd hate you a little for leaving me."

Gigi had felt badly putting her workload on Annelise for so long, but she hoped what she was about to tell her would make up for it. Gio had warned her not to tell anyone about her inheritance, but Annelise wasn't just anyone. They'd been close from the first day they'd met at boarding school. They had chosen to attend the same college, and had built their business together. When they'd first moved to Scotland, money had been tight and Annelise had been generous with what little she'd had. Annelise was like a sister to her and would remain that way regardless of how much her biological family grew.

There was no denying, though, that Gigi's life would be different now. She needed to work out what that meant, and she wanted to do it with her best friend beside her. She picked up the folder and handed it to Annelise.

"What's this?"

"Do you remember when we started this business?"

"Yes."

"And you said all you really wanted was to be able to pay off your college loans?"

Annelise nodded.

"They're paid," Gigi said, flipping open the folder on her friend's lap. "Along with the loan we took out for this building."

Annelise flipped through the paperwork, her sharp eyes missing nothing. It was one of the million reasons Gigi loved her. She didn't doubt that, had she asked Annelise, she could have quoted the total amount paid off to the penny for each receipt she was flipping through. "I don't want to sound unappreciative, Gigi, but I don't know your brothers. You shouldn't have let them pay off my bills. Yours, maybe. I mean—you're their sister. But I can't accept this."

Gigi took her friend's hand in hers. "They didn't pay your loans off. I did. There was a third possibility that neither of us considered, Annie. I had an inheritance waiting for me. A substantial one. So don't you dare not accept it."

Annelise flipped through the paid bills again. Tears filled her eyes. "It's too much, Gigi. Even if it's from you."

"You paid my rent for months when we first came here. I'm not doing more for you than you would have done for me if our situations were reversed."

"I'll pay you back. You have to be smart with money, Gigi. Even if it feels like a lot, you'd be surprised how fast it can disappear. My father used to gamble professionally, and my mother would always take half of his winnings and put it in an annuity he couldn't spend. Otherwise he could spend £50,000 just celebrating that fact he'd won £25,000. Unfortunately, after Mum died, there was no one to stop Da, and he went through everything he had in one wild binge. That's why I had to take out loans for my education. Da went through my money as well as his."

"Oh, Annelise. Why didn't you ever tell me?"

"It's not really something I brag about. Da's okay now.

He's remarried to a very nice woman who made him choose between gambling and her. Thankfully, he chose her. He might have had more money when my mum was alive, but now he sees how he got it wasn't healthy. The wins were highs for him, but the lows that followed were hard on us all."

Gigi thought about what her brothers had said about money changing people and the temptations that came with having it. It could be a blessing or a curse. She was beginning to see what they meant. "Have I told you how glad I am we're friends?"

Annelise smiled broadly. "No, but I know exactly how you feel. It's good to have you back, Gigi."

"It's good to be back," Gigi answered and closed her eyes briefly. She'd gone to the States because some questions couldn't be answered anywhere but there. And they had been. Now she was back in Edinburgh, with a new question: *Where do I go from here?* She opened her eyes and stood. "I have a project I need you to help me with."

Annelise didn't hesitate. "You'll know I'll do whatever I can."

"I want to find all the items my mother sold off and buy them back for her. It's the opposite of what we've been doing. Instead of helping people sell things, we'll be trying to buy everything back."

Wrinkling her nose, Annelise said, "Do you think they'll want to part with them? You know how collectors are."

"My mother gave up so much for me, and she shouldn't have had to." Gigi squared her shoulders with determination.

"I need to at least try."

"What does this mean for our company?"

"Do you remember how we said we'd hire an assistant if we could afford one? Let's do it. Let's get out of this office and even out of Europe. Are you game?"

"I'm in. Does you mother know about your inheritance?"

"I went to see her before I came here. I didn't tell her how much I got, but she doesn't care. She gave me the same lecture you did. She worries I'll run through it."

Annelise stood and walked to the door with Gigi. "Want to go for breakfast? I want to hear all about New York. Names. Descriptions. Everything. Especially about the part you tried to gloss over earlier. Did you really see your Mr. Zing again? How was that?"

Gigi's smile wavered. "Breakfast sounds perfect, but I don't want to talk about Kane."

They stepped out of the building together. "That doesn't sound good."

"It's not good or bad, it's nothing. Which is why I don't want to talk about it. Okay?"

Annelise linked arms with her as they walked. "Gotcha, but we do need to discuss something that's bothering me. Who comes back from a vacation thinner? Don't rich people eat? I looked at a scone yesterday, and my pants are tight today."

Gigi laughed with relief and felt the tension that had filled her at the mention of Kane's name melting away. This was Annelise; there was no reason to hide anything from her.

They hadn't made it more than a block from the office when Gigi said, "I kissed Kane again, and it was better than I remembered, and I remembered it being really, really good."

Annelise gave a skip of joy beside her. "I'm so glad we're not talking about him. Wait. Kiss? That's it? You didn't sleep with him?"

"Not even close."

Annelise let out a whistle. "Look at you, all flushed and giddy over a kiss like we're in high school. You do have it bad for this guy. So, you had enough time to get to know him while you were there. Did you date? Are you a thing now?"

"It's complicated . . ." Once Gigi started talking she couldn't stop until the whole story poured out. And because Annelise was someone who knew her better than anyone else in the world, she told her everything from how Kane had brought a date to her dinner to what she'd almost done in the coat closet that night. They both laughed until their sides hurt as Gigi described how mortified she'd been when Julia had found her.

It wasn't fun recounting how Kane had disappeared after the dinner. How she'd waited for him to contact her and had run to her phone each time it'd rung, only to be disappointed. He not only hadn't called, but he'd made himself so scarce she'd grown tired of hearing people ask where he was. Especially as her stay in the States had come to a close. Most of those who had come to welcome her had gathered again at Gio's for her goodbye dinner. Not Kane, though. Although Gigi had no proof he was deliberately avoiding her, a part of her hoped he was. She preferred to imagine him confused and holding himself back by avoiding her rather than face the much worse possibility—that he had forgotten she was even there.

By the time they found a table at a local coffee shop, Gigi forced herself to move on to happier subjects. She described how her brothers had taken time away from their work to spend time with her. How proudly they'd introduced her to more people than she could ever remember the names of. It was impossible not to smile while describing the warm welcome the entire Andrade clan had given her. Or how much they'd tried to feed her.

"So why don't you look like you ate your weight in pasta?"

"Nerves? Funny, everything was exactly what I used to dream it would be . . . in some ways even better. But I was so afraid I'd do something to mess it up or wake up and discover none of it was real."

"Good things are possible, Gigi. Statistically, they have to happen to someone eventually."

"I like the way you look at this. Not as a nearly impossible occurrence, but as somehow destined if enough bad shit happens to everyone else."

Annelise smiled. "That's not exactly what I mean, but close. So, aren't you glad you finally broke down and met your brothers?"

Gigi swirled her coffee around her cup. "I am. We're still figuring each other out, but I'm not angry anymore. At least, not with them."

"Do you wish you'd gone earlier?"

"No. I wasn't ready. I don't think they were either. I get the feeling things with them weren't always the way they are now. They want me to be one of them, but they don't want me to ask questions. I know them, but I don't. Does that make sense?"

"That sounds about right. At least, in my experience. People have secrets, Gigi, and the older I get the more I'm beginning to think it's better not to know them." Annelise gave Gigi a long look. "There's more, though, isn't there? Something is bothering you."

Gigi looked down at the paper napkin she'd been absently folding and creasing in her hands. "When I told you about Kane the first time, you said connections like that aren't real. That's not the way it felt, Annelise. I can't stop thinking about him, no matter how much I tell myself I should stop. Why would he kiss me the way he did and then walk away? I don't understand."

"Have you considered calling him?"

"And saying what? Hello, is there any chance you like me and haven't gotten around to acting on it yet? If he had any interest in me, he'd call me, right?"

"How good was that kiss?"

"Un-fucking-believable."

"He'll call."

"Three weeks ago, I would have agreed with you. Now, I don't think so."

"I'd say you have a ninety-seven-point-three percent chance of hearing from him again."

Gigi laughed. It felt good to make light of something that had weighed heavily upon her thoughts for weeks. "Not one hundred?"

Annelise smirked. "When it comes to men, you always have to leave a small margin for the possibility of utter stupidity."

✧   ✧   ✧

"Well, at least you're still alive," Nick Andrade said from the doorway of Kane's office a few weeks later.

Kane turned with a groan. "What do need, Nick?"

Nick plopped down in one of his office chairs and propped his feet up on the table in front of it. "Rena sent me. She's worried about you. No one has seen you in a while."

Kane walked over and knocked Nick's feet from the table. "I've been working a lot. It looks like we're adding a new satellite office in Europe."

Nick put his feet back up on the table and grinned in challenge. "I know, your father told me at dinner on Sunday. The dinner you said you'd go to but didn't."

Kane took a deep breath. "I don't have time for this. Tell my sister I'm fine. I'll come to dinner this weekend."

Nick folded his arms across his chest. "Rena thinks you're sulking over Gigi. Is that true?"

Kane glared at him, but said nothing.

With a widening grin, Nick stood. "You are. And I love the poetic justice of it. You gave me a lot of shit for falling for your little sister. I hope Gio is more understanding than you were." When Kane still said nothing, Nick snapped his fingers and pointed. "He doesn't know, though, does he? Please let me be there when you tell him."

Kane turned away and put the distance of half the room between them. He felt the urge to hit something coming on and didn't want to have to explain to Rena how her husband's face met his fist. He looked out the window and said, "Never going to happen, because there is nothing to tell."

Nick joined him by the window. "Yet. Women have a funny way of making men do things they normally never would do. Even take a morning out of work to check in on their condescending brother-in-law who doesn't have the balls to admit he might be human like the rest of us."

Kane slammed his fist sideways against the wall beside him. He'd avoided his family for this very reason. His ache for Gigi was strengthening instead of lessening. As he caught a glimpse of his own reflection in the window, he saw a man he didn't like. First he'd told himself he was staying away from Gigi because she was Gio's little sister. Then he'd maintained that Gigi's relationship with her brothers was more important than his desire to have her. However, a battle was raging within him, and it was one he was losing.

He woke each morning with an image of her in his mind. The pain in her eyes when she'd seen him with Lynn. *I am such an ass.* The soft moan she'd made when he'd kissed her on the porch, and the ache of what could have been reality. *Gigi in my bed. In my arms.*

The man he saw in his reflection was a hypocrite. He wasn't staying away from Gigi because he cared about her relationship with her brothers. His decision no longer had anything to do with how Gio would feel.

Gigi had become an obsession.

He knew if he went to her, there would be no turning back. No halfway. She would be his, regardless of what it cost either of them.

After a short pause, Nick added, "Gigi's back in Scotland."

Kane kept his eyes on the New York skyline. "I know." Unable to stop himself, Kane asked, "How is she handling everything?"

"Better. The shock has passed. It's a big life change, but she seems to be working through it."

"Good."

"She said she'd be back for another visit soon. I'm going to miss her. It was nice having a little sister around."

Kane nodded.

"Rena told me how you went through a bottle of Scotch and gushed about Gigi to your father. How you thought her name was Luisella, the woman you'd been looking for since our wedding."

Kane took a deep breath. "Rena talks too much."

Without missing a beat, Nick added, "Only when she cares. We both think you should go to Scotland."

Kane walked to his desk and picked up a report he'd printed to show his team. "I don't get you, Nick. I can't tell if you're here because you actually care or because you like starting trouble."

Nick shook his head slowly in disgust. "Stop trying to

figure me out, and ask yourself why you've moved into your office and have quit talking to your family and friends. If it's Gigi, you're a fool if you pass up something with her because you think Gio won't approve. You don't have to worry about him. Treat her well, and he'll get over it. Fuck with her, and I'll kill you first. See? Problem solved, either way. Go to Scotland."

As Nick began to saunter away, Kane called out, "Nick."

Nick stopped at the door and looked over his shoulder.

"Thanks for coming by."

Nick smiled and walked out of the office.

Kane stood beside his desk. He absently rolled the folder in his hand and tapped it against the open palm of his other.

Gigi.

What would she do if he flew to Scotland?

He knew what he hoped she'd do, and the idea had his cock stirring even as he walked out of his office. They would share so much more than a kiss. He wanted to claim her, slowly, all night long . . . wake the next day and start all over again.

He stopped in the hallway just before the conference room and took several calming breaths. His cock was at full attention, which was no way to run a meeting.

He pictured her sweet lips closing over his cock while he ran his hands through her hair and that was enough to destroy the last of his resistance. He called his secretary and told her to clear his schedule for the rest of the day, including the meeting he'd called. "Tell them something unavoidable came up." Kane inwardly groaned at his choice of words. "Arrange a car to pick me up at my apartment in an hour, and call my pilot. Have him meet me at the airport."

"Where should I tell him you're going?" Marge asked.

"Scotland. Edinburgh to be exact."

"Thank God," Marge said under her breath, confirming that Rena did, indeed, talk too much about his personal business.

It was impossible to be irritated with either, though. Nick was right. Rena only got involved when she cared, and Marge had been with the company longer than Kane. She was practically family. She'd originally worked for his father and was not only reliable, but was so integral to the running of the office he often took her for granted. That said, he knew the first call she'd make. Kane decided to use it to his advantage rather than balk at it. "Update my father on the Whittle files. I'll be meeting with our European teams while I'm over there. He'll love covering for me while I'm gone."

Marge added cheerfully, "Tell Gigi I said hi."

Kane almost denied that he would see her, but there was no reason to try to keep secret what was apparently already a well-discussed topic. "I will," Kane said, his footsteps becoming lighter as he went. Maybe he'd been a fool to fight his feelings for as long as he had. No one seemed to have a problem with it except him.

A few hours later, Kane was flying over the Atlantic in his private jet. Even though he'd been sporting a grin since he'd made his decision, he knew there was one last thing he had to do.

He took out his cell phone and called Gio. It went directly to voice mail. Kane left a brief message stating he was headed to London for business and intended to stop in to see Gigi while in the area.

It was a more appropriate announcement than he would have left had he decided to be completely honest. *Gio, I'm heading off for what I hope is a deliciously, decadent romp with your sister. Talk to you soon.*

Chapter Thirteen

"WHAT AN ASSHOLE," Gigi stormed as she entered her apartment with Annelise. She threw her purse down on the table and kicked off her high heels before padding to her cupboard. "I need wine. How about you? Red or white?"

"Whatever you have," Annelise called back from the living room.

Gigi returned with two glasses and a bottle of merlot. She poured wine for both of them, placed the bottle on the table between them, and sank into the comfort of her couch. "I hate people."

Annelise kicked off her own shoes and curled up on the chair across from her, sipping her wine as she did. "Don't let one man represent an entire species."

"He didn't even consider our offer. What does he mean, 'it's priceless'? He bought it. Which means it had a price. What's the use of having money if I can't use it for what's important?"

"You said Gio and Julia are flying in tomorrow morning, right? Maybe they'll have a suggestion. Who knows, they might even know him."

"I can't ask Gio to help me with this."

"Why not?"

"It goes into that sticky, emotionally charged area we avoid. I'd have to explain why my mother sold the items off, Gio would feel guilty about not knowing I existed, and somehow we'd end up right back in the place where no one was right and everyone feels badly about things we can't do anything about now."

"Except, make amends, which Gio could do by helping you with this."

"It's not worth the conversation." As soon as the words were out of her mouth, she rethought them. "Not unless it's the only way. Then, you're right, making the palazzo whole again for my mother is . . . as Mr. Wentforth said, priceless."

Gigi's cell phone buzzed with a message. "It's Rocco. Oh, my God." Gigi jumped up from her spot on the couch and knocked her glass of wine over on the table. "Shit."

Annelise was beside her, mopping up the mess with napkins. "What happened? What did he say?"

Gigi read over the message from her bodyguard again. "He said Kane is here. In my apartment building. Right downstairs. Why would he come here?"

Annelise walked over to pick up her purse. "Because he wants to see you?"

"Where are you going?" Gigi asked in a panic and read another message on her phone. "Rocco said Kane is on his way up."

"You don't want me here."

Gigi grabbed her friend's arm. "Yes, I do. You don't know how I get with Kane. I can't be alone with him."

Thoroughly amused, Annelise asked, "Are you afraid he'll jump you or that you'll jump him?"

Gigi's grip tightened on Annelise's arm. "Neither. Both. I don't know. I need your objective opinion. Stay and watch how he is with me. I don't even care if this sounds immature. I'm telling you, my brain shuts off around him. Help me not make a complete fool of myself by imagining what's maybe not there."

Laughing, Annelise pried Gigi's hand off her arm. "Okay. Okay. I'll hang out for a little bit. I've never seen you like this with a man."

"I've never felt like this. I'm already a wreck. Imagine how I'd be if I slept with him and then didn't hear from him. I'd go insane."

"Whoa, where did that come from? Slow down. You barely know him, and the last time you saw him he was with another woman."

"I know. Which is why you have to swear to stay. I can't trust my judgment when it comes to Kane. Whatever happens, don't leave." There was a knock on the door. "Promise?"

Concern had replaced Annelise's amusement. "I promise. I don't want you to get hurt, Gigi."

Gigi gave Annelise a quick hug, then checked her image in a mirror on the wall before rushing to the door. "I don't want that either. Especially since he's so close to Gio. I don't want to do anything that threatens what I found, but, oh, wait until you see him."

With her heart thudding crazily in her chest and her hands shaking with excitement, Gigi tried to keep her facial expression calm when she opened the door. "Kane, this is a surprise." Her eyes flew to his, and the chemistry she'd asked herself a thousand times if she'd imagined was back, even stronger than before. Her lips parted involuntarily, and she swallowed nervously. He leaned in as if drawn by the same irresistible force. His lips hovered above hers, the warmth of his breath a caress she knew she'd enjoy on many parts of her. Flushed, Gigi licked her bottom lip and loved how he watched the move hungrily.

"I hope I'm not interrupting anything," he said in a deep, husky voice.

"We were just having wine," Annelise said from beside them. "You must be Kane. My name is Annelise."

Kane raised his head slowly and tore his eyes from Gigi to greet her friend. "Yes, I am. It's a pleasure to meet you."

Gigi clung to the door handle for support, practically sagging against it during the temporary reprieve. *I'm such an idiot. For all I know Gio asked him to drop something off for me. Hold it together.* "What brings you by, Kane?"

His eyes flew back to hers, as they silently said, "You." But his actual answer gave much less away. "I have business in London. I didn't see you before you left and thought I'd check to see how you're doing."

Breathe. Play it cool. Gigi closed the door and raised a hand in the direction of the couches behind them. "Well, your timing is perfect. As Annelise said, we were just having wine. Would you like a glass?"

"I'd love one." It wasn't what Kane said, but how he said it that sent waves of heat through Gigi. He wanted more than wine.

Oh, God, me too. Me, too. "Have a seat. I'll get you a glass."

Behind the swinging door of her kitchen, Gigi wrapped her arms around her waist, closed her eyes, and bit her lip. *I don't know him well enough to feel this way. If being ditched after a kiss hurt, do I really want to risk more?*

Don't do it.

✧   ✧   ✧

WHEN GIGI RETURNED with his glass, Kane was seated on the couch across from her friend. The way Annelise was looking him over reminded him how he'd felt in high school when going out with someone involved meeting her father. He shot her what he considered a charming smile.

She didn't smile back. "So, how long will you be in London?"

"London?"

Her eyes narrowed. "You said you were here for business."

"Oh, yes. Not sure yet. We're considering an expansion, so I'm visiting sites for a potential secondary regional office."

"Any in Scotland?"

"Very possibly."

"Would it be a permanent office or a temporary endeavor?"

Kane loosened the tie that suddenly felt tight around his neck. He stood with relief when Gigi returned with his glass of wine and one for herself. The awkwardness of Annelise's questions was quickly forgotten as well as the woman herself. That was the risk of seeing Gigi again. He wanted her with an intensity that overshadowed everything and everyone.

Gigi held out the glass of wine to Kane. His hand brushed hers while he accepted it. From the expression in her eyes when they met his, Kane knew she felt the same fire that had shot through him. "Thank you," he said softly. She held his eyes for a moment longer. He'd never wanted to kiss a woman as desperately as he wanted to kiss her. To taste her plump lips. He groaned.

"Gigi, Kane was just telling me about the business that brought him to the area. It sounds as if it's all still up in the air," Annelise said cheerfully from the chair across from them.

Without looking at her friend, Gigi answered breathlessly, "Business decisions can be complicated. They aren't something to be rushed into."

"Not unless you know what you want and, in this case, I do," Kane said.

"Do you?" Gigi's lips parted again deliciously.

"Yes," Kane said decisively.

Annelise chirped in again. "How exciting. And surprising, I bet, too. Gigi, didn't you tell me you hadn't heard from Kane since you saw him that last time at Gio's?"

Gigi shook her head as if clearing it, and the temporary spell that had overtaken both of them was broken. She looked over at her friend and nodded. "I did say that."

They seemed to share a meaningful look. "You did."

Gigi took a seat in a chair beside the couch and downed a gulp of her wine. Kane placed his glass on the table in front of him and returned to the couch. He turned a charming smile on Annelise again. "Do you think it's possible to give Gigi and me a few minutes alone? We have something we need to . . . discuss."

He expected Annelise to bow out gracefully. She seemed to understand what was going on between them. However, in an act that raised Kane's level of frustration, Annelise settled herself deeper in her chair. "Gigi and I tell each other everything, so I'm sure she's okay with me hearing whatever."

"It's okay, Annelise. I want to hear what he has to say."

"That's apparent, but I promised to hang out with you tonight. Remember how you said you didn't want to be alone?"

"She won't be," Kane said definitively. He had no intention of leaving. Gigi's eyes flew to his.

"Annelise is right. She should stay."

Okay. Gigi had called in reinforcements. That was fair. *Why should she trust me? I haven't given her a reason to. I imagine she's as confused as I have been.* Kane stood and walked over to Gigi. "I spent the last month living at my office instead of coming here and doing what I wanted to." He took her by the hand and pulled her up to stand in front of him. "This."

The moment their lips touched all sanity left Kane.

What started as a light kiss deepened quickly. Gigi wound her arms around his neck, pressing intimately against him. He couldn't get enough. She held nothing back. It was a kiss that consumed both of them.

"Okay, that's it. I give up. It was nice to meet you, Kane. Gigi, call me tomorrow." With that, Annelise left the apartment.

Kane heard her, but he was already beyond caring about her presence. Gigi felt better than he remembered. Her mouth tasted sweeter. Her body softer beneath his firm hands. He didn't want to stop to discuss why he hadn't contacted her.

Without breaking off their kiss he lifted her in his arms and set off down the hallway toward what he guessed would be her bedroom. He'd spent countless nights imagining what he would do if he had Gigi in his bed.

Tonight he planned to enjoy every moment of being in hers.

Chapter Fourteen

YEARS OF FANTASIZING about Kane added to what was already a sexually charged walk to Gigi's bedroom. Somewhere in the back of her head she heard her own voice telling her to slow down, but she ignored it. Her hands ran hungrily across his strong shoulders. She opened her mouth wider to his hot tongue. He was a warrior, laying claim to her body, and she was his *very eager* spoils of war.

He laid her across her bed more gently than his deep kiss implied he would, and Gigi shook with excitement. He stood over her, lust burning in his eyes, as he looked her over slowly, savoring her, even clothed. "I've wanted this since the first time we met."

Breathing beneath the heat of his gaze was difficult. Gigi was practically squirming with the need for his mouth on her again, to feel his hands on her bare skin. She raised herself and brought her hands to the top button of her blouse. His nostrils flared. She slowly undid each button, loving how he didn't hide his obvious excitement at watching her. It gave her a boldness she didn't normally have in the bedroom. She felt beautiful and sexy beyond anything she'd experienced before; the feeling was addictive.

She dropped her blouse to the floor beside the bed and unclasped her bra, slipping it off and dropping that too beside the bed. His cheeks flushed pink. Gigi went up onto her knees and moved to the edge of the bed before him.

Their ragged breathing was the only sound in the room until he groaned and bent to take one of her breasts into his mouth. Gigi placed her hands on his shoulders and threw her head back as he skillfully teased and circled her nipple. He adored her with his tongue, his teeth, and the sweet hotness of his breath. She writhed in pleasure against his mouth, loving how his fingers played softly with her other breast. He kissed his way across her chest to her other breast and started his erotic assault all over again. Before Kane, Gigi would have said she liked to have her breasts kissed, but she had no idea it could feel like this.

Holy shit.

When his teeth closed over her hardened nipple and gave it a little tug, Gigi cried out in pleasure and nearly came. Even though his touch was concentrated to one area, Gigi's entire body was on fire. Beneath her skirt, her silk panties were soaked. She wanted his cock inside her with a frenzied need that could no longer be suppressed.

She reached for the belt of his pants, but he stilled her hands. "Not yet."

With one strong move he lifted her so she was standing on the low bed in front of him. The substantial height difference between them brought her breasts in perfect alignment with his mouth. As he once again began to kiss her, his hands caressed the outside of her thighs, up her skirt until he found the waistband of her panties. He slid them down gently. Gigi kept a hand on his shoulder for support while she stepped out of them. He pushed her skirt up so it bunched around her waist and brought his mouth down to kiss her mound. "Perfect. So fucking perfect," he said against her trimmed sex.

His eyes sought hers, and Gigi had never felt more beautiful. One of his hands ran warmly from the back of her knee to cup the curve of her ass in a proprietary move. He guided her legs to a more open stance, then his fingers dove between her wet folds, seeking her sensitive nub.

Gigi grasped both sides of his face and lowered her mouth to his. She drove her tongue between his lips, claiming him as he claimed her. There was no thought beyond the pleasure of his touch, beyond the need that pulsed through her. She was humming for him, an instrument happily being played by its exceptionally talented musician.

Gigi gasped into his mouth when the first wave of her climax shook through her. Kane broke off their kiss, and the movement of his fingers across her clit increased in rhythm. Gigi's eyes began to close, but Kane gave the back of her ass a light slap. It didn't hurt, but it was enough of a surprise that Gigi's eyes flew open. Kane growled, "Don't look away. You're so wet. So ready. Come for me, Gigi."

Giving herself over to him was pleasure in itself. Gigi gripped his shoulders and held his eyes as wave after wave of orgasm shuddered through her. When she thought it couldn't get better, he slid two fingers inside her and began to pump in and out with a force that prolonged her climax and had her crying out his name while begging him not to stop.

He didn't. Not until she slumped slightly against him. Then he turned her before him, unclasped her skirt and lowered it until she shakily stepped out of that too. Completely naked, she turned back toward him, flushed and ready for whatever he wanted.

He stepped out of his shoes, threw his tie on the floor, pulled his shirt from his trousers, up over his head, and threw it to the floor. Without looking away from her, he undid his belt and stepped out of the rest of his clothing. Gigi's eyes wantonly sought what she craved. His shaft was fully erect and a mouth-watering size.

Without warning he grabbed both of her calves and pulled them out from beneath her. She fell with a whoosh onto the bed behind her, leaving her spread-eagled before him on the bed. She would have laughed at the joy of his confident roughness, but she met his eyes, and her need for him seared through her. There was nothing funny about how close she was to begging him to take her.

He rolled on a condom then moved above her. His hands were everywhere on her, strong and bold. She ran her hands over every part of him she could reach. Kissed his chest, his neck, his lips when he brought his mouth near hers. Theirs was a mating he commanded, but Gigi loved every minute of it.

When he eased the tip of his shaft between her folds, Gigi opened wide for him. He dipped just an inch into her eager sex, then pulled out and slid himself up and down across her clit before dipping inside her again.

He adjusted himself onto his elbows and cupped her face as he kissed her deeply. The thrust of his tongue grew deeper, synchronizing with the thrust of his cock. Gigi met both with everything in her, finding joy in giving herself fully to him.

His thrusts grew more forceful, filling her beyond what she'd known. He moved to adjust her hips, lifting her legs to allow a more fulfilling depth. The careful skill and gentleness of his lovemaking gave way to a wilder mating. She felt the change in him, and it was an aphrodisiac like none other. He was a man who was always in control, but with her, he was as much a slave to her desire as she was to his.

She came with that thought blissfully accompanying the cascading fire that rocked through her. He joined her with fierce, deep thrusts and a primal, "Mine."

He gave her a final, hot kiss and rolled onto his side beside her to dispose of the condom before pulling her back into his arms. She wrapped her sweaty body around his and closed her eyes. Whatever the future held for them, Annelise had been wrong about one important thing—*the zing* was real.

More real than she had even imagined.

✧ ✧ ✧

KANE PULLED A bed sheet over Gigi, surprised by how protective he felt over her. The sex between them had shaken him with its intensity. There was no going back to how things were before. She was his now. How their relationship would play out was as uncertain as what the consequences of it would be. None of that mattered to him, though. He would overcome any obstacle as long as it meant she would remain in his arms and in his bed.

I sound like a caveman. He kissed Gigi's forehead and smiled at her when her eyes fluttered open at his touch. *I feel like one whenever she looks at me.*

Her smile was shy, which was adorable after the intimacy they'd shared. "Hi," she said.

He kissed her nose. "Hi, yourself."

"I did not mean for that to happen," she joked.

He nuzzled her neck. "I did."

She raised a hand and placed it over her eyes. "Tell me Annelise left before you carried me in here."

He kissed his way to just behind her ear. "You don't remember?"

She chuckled, still covering her eyes. "No. Oh, my God. I've never done anything like this before."

He bit her earlobe gently and growled, "Never?"

She lowered her hand. "I'm not saying I was a vir—" She stopped and her eyes narrowed at the smile she caught on his face. "You're teasing me."

He rolled onto his back, taking her with him so she was sprawled across him. The feel of her soft thighs brushing against his cock had him already hardening again. He moved her so she could feel him along her still wet lower lips. "Maybe. But, you like it, don't you?"

Gigi sat up, moving herself along his shaft in an intimate,

hot caress. "Is there any point in trying to pretend I don't?"

He slipped the bare tip of his cock deeper between her lips. She kissed him deeply while wiggling against him, driving him nearly out of control. He broke off the kiss and ordered huskily, "Lean over and grab the last condom from my pants pocket."

Her eyes sparkled with lust and humor. "Last? You only brought two?"

"I knew one wouldn't be enough. Three seemed presumptuous."

She laid a hand flat on the middle of his chest and frowned down at him. "I don't know if I like that you brought them at all. I might have said no."

He reached up, took her by the arms, and pulled her down onto him, claiming her mouth with his. He kissed her deeply. He didn't want to try to put how he was feeling into words. When he broke off the kiss, he said, "Get the damn condom before I take you without it."

She moved off him to retrieve what he requested and rolled it onto his cock. Instead of instantly returning to her previous position, she knelt beside him, looking into his eyes. "What is it about you that makes me want to say yes every time?"

Kane ran a hand up one of her firm thighs, up her slim waist, and gently brushed the side of her breast with the back of his hand. "I don't know, but I've felt the same from the first time we kissed. You were too young then, but I wanted to say yes to you then. And it was torture to stay away from you in New York."

"Then why did you?" Her eyes were wide and full of uncertainty.

"I told myself it was better for all of us if I did."

"Not because you were with that woman from the party?"

Kane closed his eyes for a moment. It was difficult to have the conversation while his cock was throbbing for release. "She's a friend."

"The kind with benefits?"

"Before the party, yes. But not after I kissed you that night. You've haunted me since then, Gigi."

She smiled, her eyes twinkling with satisfaction. "Good."

Kane leaned upward, slipped a hand behind Gigi's neck and pulled her back down on top of him. "We can talk later. Right now, all I can think about is fucking you until neither of us can move."

She laughed softly against him, an act that jiggled her amazing tits back and forth across his chest. "That might be tough with only one condom left."

He rolled them both over until he was between her thighs with his cock poised above her sex. "Challenge accepted," he growled. He had all night to show her how many other ways they could make each other come.

Chapter Fifteen

THE NEXT MORNING Gigi woke to the sound of her phone ringing in the living room. She reached for Kane instinctively, and was disappointed to discover the bed beside her was empty. Disappointment dissolved quickly, however, when she realized the sound in the background was the shower. He wasn't gone. And last night had actually happened.

She rolled and stretched like a cat in the sun, loving how sated she felt. Kane had worshipped every inch of her last night and the memories brought a smile to her lips that could not be denied. Annelise was probably checking in on her. Gigi let the call ring through. Annelise would be full of questions Gigi wasn't ready to face yet. She didn't want to think about the future or if she and Kane had one. She wanted to savor every moment of being with him. And if Kane wanted nothing more than sex? She'd deal with that as soon as the perma-grin faded from her face. A woman could be pardoned for wanting a repeat of last night more than she wanted to analyze it.

Her phone started ringing again. Gigi threw back the bed

sheets, reached for a robe, and padded to the living room to answer it. "Hello?"

She nearly dropped the phone when it was Julia, Gio's wife. "Gigi, you can tell us to come back later, but Gio and I arrived early, and we wanted to take you out for breakfast."

Gigi sat on one of the chairs in shock. "Arrived? You're in Edinburgh already?" With everything that had happened, Gigi had completely forgotten her brother and sister-in-law had said they were coming for a visit.

"We're downstairs. Gio is grilling your bodyguard. I hope you wanted overprotective brothers, because that's what you got. Gio's so excited to see you, too. It's sweet. I told him you'd be at work by now, and we could wait until tonight to see you, but he called your office and when Annelise said you weren't coming in today he became worried. You're not sick, are you?"

"No, I'm fine. I was up late last night and decided to sleep in today. I'm still pretty tired. Do you mind if we meet up later today?" Gigi looked behind her at the bedroom door in panic. This wasn't how she wanted Gio to find out about her and Kane.

"See, Gio. I told you she's okay, just tired." Gio said something to Julia Gigi didn't catch, and Julia answered, "No, she does not have a man up there. And even if she did, it's none of your business. She's twenty-five."

Gigi cringed when she heard Gio's answer. "It is my business. She's my sister."

Julia sighed. "Oh boy, Gigi. Do you have anyone up there?"

Gigi lied under the pressure. "No; like I said, I'm just tired."

"Gio, she's alone. You're getting all worked up over nothing. Gigi, he's not like this normally. He thinks now you have your inhcritance you're ripe for someone trying to scam you." Julia had a quiet conversation with her husband that was unintelligible to Gigi before speaking into the phone again. "Are you dressed, because your brother is being paranoid? He thinks your bodyguard looks guilty. Now he's worried you may be held hostage up there and unable to tell us. Oh, my God, Gio. Stop. Can we come up for a minute, Gigi? Then I promise you, this will never happen again. Right, Gio?"

Gigi stood and started to pace her small living room. "You can't come up. You have to convince Gio to leave because I do have someone here."

Julia made a sound of understanding. "Oh, crap. I wish I were a good liar. About what? Gio, I can't tell you. We're leaving though, and we'll see Gigi tonight as we had originally planned. You do still want to see us tonight?"

Gigi closed her eyes briefly and answered quietly, "Yes."

"See? All is good. Let's go, Gio."

After hanging up, Gigi sagged back against the chair in relief. If she wasn't ready to explain last night to Annelise, she definitely wasn't prepared to defend it to Gio. She owed Julia a grateful hug the next time she saw her for diffusing what might have been an ugly situation.

A loud knock on the door was followed by Gio's voice ordering, "Open the door, Gigi."

Gigi stood, tightened the belt of her robe around her waist and reluctantly opened the door enough so she could see her brother. He looked as angry as his wife was embarrassed.

With a sheepish smile, Julia poked around Gio's side and said, "I'm sorry, Gigi, I tried. He can be so stubborn sometimes."

Eyes narrowed with irritation, Gio said, "Rocco wouldn't look me in the eye when I asked him why you had stayed home. He wouldn't tell me who was with you, either. He's gone."

Good for Rocco! Anger slowly overtook Gigi's embarrassment. "You can't fire my bodyguard."

Gio looked back at her like a king explaining his role. "I can if I hired him."

"Something you shouldn't have done because I told you I didn't need one."

"Then you won't miss him."

Gigi threw up her hands in frustration, and the door swung the rest of the way open as she did. "Gio, I'm your sister, but I'm not a child. I am perfectly capable of—"

"Who's at the door, Gigi?" Kane asked from behind her. She looked over her shoulder just in time to see Kane walk fully into the living room with a white towel slung around his waist and another towel draped around his neck. She tried to wave him back, but it was too late.

"Kane?" Gio bellowed as he stepped past Gigi and into her apartment and strode toward Kane.

Julia went to stand beside Gigi. "Maybe it won't be so

bad. They've known each other for most of their lives. They're like brothers. They'll work it out."

Gio stood face to face with Kane, his fists clenched at his sides. "I trusted you, Kane."

"I understand why you're angry, Gio. I didn't plan for this to happen. Trust me, I tried to stay away from her."

"It doesn't look like you tried fucking hard enough."

Gigi went to stand beside the two men. "Don't fight over me."

Neither one of them acknowledged her. "I met Gigi at your wedding. I walked away from her then, but I never forgot her. When I found out she was your sister, I didn't want to want her."

"Tell me this isn't because Nick married your sister. You wouldn't do something like this out of spite, would you?"

"You know me better than that."

"I thought I did."

Julia went to stand beside Gio. She placed a hand on his arm. "Gio, this isn't the time to talk about this."

"You're right," Gio growled. "It looks like I waited too long to tell my best friend my sister was off limits."

"Kane? Gio?" When neither responded, Gigi stuck out her chin defiantly. "Can either of you hear me?"

Kane didn't back down in the face of Gio's anger, nor did he spare Gigi a glance. "I understand this is a shock, Gio."

Gio ran a hand angrily through his hair. "Just tell me you have real feelings for her . . ."

Kane said, "I—"

Gigi raised her voice to an ear-deafening pitch. "Enough."

Kane and Gio turned to look at her in surprise. She waved finger at both of them. "Gio, you do not get to tell me who I can or can't be with. And, Kane, don't you dare say you feel something for me because my brother told you to. I want both of you to leave my apartment—now."

Julia walked over to the still-open door and pointed to the hallway on the other side. "I agree. I think the two of you need to go cool off. Gigi, I'm sorry. I've never seen Gio behave this way."

"Me?" Gio asked in arrogant surprise.

Julia waved a hand angrily in the air. "Yes, you. I love you, but I'm mortified right now. Please respect your sister's request and leave."

"There is no way—" Gio stopped talking when he realized how upset his wife was. "You can't expect me to pretend to be happy about this."

Julia shook her head and pointed toward the door again. "No, but I do expect you to listen to what your sister is saying, and she's asking you to leave."

Gio took a step toward the door, frowned, assessed his wife's determination, then began walking again.

"You, too, Kane."

Kane looked to Gigi in confusion. Gigi folded her arms across her chest. "Thank you, Julia. I'm glad they can hear one of us."

With his face set in harsh lines, Kane said, "I'm not leaving like this."

Gio snapped, "You're not staying."

Kane and Gio faced off again near the door. "I value our friendship, Gio, but this is something you will have to accept because—"

"Get out," Gigi yelled. Julia helped them along with a not-so-gentle physical nudge and slammed the door behind them.

"I'm in a towel," Kane announced as if that would have the two women throwing the door open.

Julia's eyes filled with amusement, and she raised a hand to her mouth to hide her smile.

Some of Gigi's anger lessened at the ridiculousness of a half-naked Kane in the hallway with Gio. Gigi met Julia's eyes and said loudly, "You should have thought of that before you made me too angry to let you back in."

In a voice that sounded as though he was trying to reason with a child, Kane said, "Gigi, my phone and my wallet are in there. I couldn't leave even if I wanted to."

Gigi walked to the floor of the bedroom, picked up Kane's clothing, and strode to the door. Julia opened the door just wide enough to allow Gigi to throw the clothing out before closing the door again.

In a much more humble tone, Gio asked, "Julia, I'm heading back to the hotel. Are you coming with me?"

"No," Julia answered firmly. "Gigi and I are going to have a nice quiet breakfast together. We'll probably go shopping after that. Tonight we'll have dinner at The Witchery because I've been looking forward to eating there. If you and Kane can work out your differences before then, you can both join us. If not, I intend to have a nice meal with my sister-in-law."

"Julia . . ."

"I'll see you tonight, Gio."

Gigi walked over and hugged Julia. She whispered, "You are amazing."

Julia hugged her back and said softly, "They are both wonderful men, but just like most people, they will only treat you as well as you demand to be treated. You were right to ask them to leave. That was not them at their best, and they know it. Or they will once they've had time to think about it."

◆ ◆ ◆

"Why am I out here with you?" Kane asked in irritation as he bent to pick up his clothing off the floor, a move that almost caused him to lose the towel from his waist. He cinched it tighter at his hip.

Gio was shaking his head in shock. "I can't believe Julia threw me out. She doesn't get angry like that."

Kane tucked the clothing beneath one of his arms. "Well, you were ignoring her when she tried to talk to you."

Gio glared at Kane. "Oh, I'm sorry, I must have been distracted by . . . oh, I don't know . . . maybe the fact you're fucking my baby sister."

"She's twenty-five, Gio. She's not a baby. Not even close. And you should talk about her with more respect. She's not just any woman to me. I have feelings for her."

"And you think that makes it better?"

"No," Kane said in frustration. "I know it doesn't. I remember how I felt when I found out about Nick and Rena. I wanted to wring his neck. Punch me; go ahead. I won't even block it. I deserve the hit, but that doesn't change how I feel about Gigi."

Gio looked his friend over and made a face. "I can't hit you when you're standing there in just a towel. Put some damn clothes on."

"That didn't stop you back in high school when you thought you caught me with the girl you had a crush on."

Gio smiled wryly at the memory. He flexed his right hand as if remembering the punch. "I didn't know she had a twin." He frowned. "And you were wrong that time, too."

"You didn't date her before or after anyway."

"I couldn't. You had ruined her for me. All I could picture when I looked at her was you in a Scooby-Doo towel." Gio shuddered.

"Whatever, man. Ancient history. You're lucky I saved you from those twins. They wouldn't have stood up to you the way Julia does. In the end, I did you a favor."

"I can't go on a double date tonight with you and my sister."

"Good, because I don't want to have dinner with you. As soon as that door opens, Gigi and I are going to have a long talk. I'll explain to her that you meant well."

"I don't need you to explain me to my own sister."

"Then why are you out here in the hall instead of in there?"

"You're fucking out here with me."

"I can't believe she threw me out. You'd think after the night we had—"

Gio's face went white with anger. "Say one more word and I have to hit you."

Kane shrugged. "Sorry, but you know what I mean."

Between gritted teeth, Gio said, "I know exactly what you mean. That's the problem."

The two of them stood in tense silence for several minutes.

Gio finally said, "I don't think they're going to open the door."

Kane looked down at the towel around him. "I should probably get dressed. There must be a public bathroom in this building."

"I saw one downstairs."

Kane pressed the button on the elevator across the hall. When the car arrived they both stepped inside. His stomach rumbled loudly. "I need coffee."

Without softening his harsh expression, Gio said, "There's a breakfast place at the end of the block. Julia and I were going to take Gigi there."

Kane assessed his friend with a sideways glance. "Do you want to get something to eat?"

Gio growled, "Only because I'm starving, not because I'm okay with any part of what just happened."

Finally, something we agree on.

Chapter Sixteen

As Gigi and Julia walked up the cobblestoned Royal Mile toward the famous Witchery restaurant, stopping in the touristy shops along the way, Gigi's tension rose. Until then, Julia had kept her mind off the morning's drama. Her sister-in-law was hilarious and very down-to-earth. It was also fun seeing the city through her eyes.

Until a few moments ago, Gigi had been laughing until her sides hurt. Julia had dragged her to Camera Obscura where they had gone floor to floor playing with the illusion exhibits. It was impossible to be in a bad mood while watching Julia stick her head through a special table that made it look as if her head were being served on a platter.

The easy part of the day was over, though. Julia led Gigi into one last store, then it was off to meet the men for dinner. Gigi voiced her concern. "What happens if they don't come?"

Julia put the Loch Ness T-shirt she'd been looking at back on the shelf and answered confidently, "They will."

Gigi absently felt the material of a display kilt. "I know Gio will because you're there, but Kane?"

Julia turned toward Gigi and put a hand on her arm. "You can tell me I'm overstepping, but I have to say something. Everything I know about you, your mother, and how you were raised away from your brothers makes me admire you more. You didn't have it easy, but look what you did with your life. You're amazing even without any of us. Don't forget that. Gio will come to dinner just as much for you as he will for me. He loves you unconditionally. And you deserve to be loved like that, even if you don't believe it yet. I don't know if Kane does or doesn't have deep feelings for you, but you are amazing without him, too. Don't forget that. If he doesn't see that yet, show him. Don't make everything so easy for him that he doesn't see the value in you."

Gigi wasn't sure how to take Julia's advice. "Are you telling me to play harder to get?"

Julia picked the Loch Ness shirt back up and laid it over her arm. "No, I'm telling you to remember that you are a beautiful, intelligent woman, and he needs to respect that if he's going to be with you. When you deal with men who spend their days in command of their financial empires, they can forget to turn that off when they come home. A good man will wake up when given a gentle reminder. Don't settle for less than a good man, Gigi. No matter who he is."

They walked to the register to buy the black shirt with a wanted poster for the infamous lake monster. Gigi was still digesting what Julia had said, so she focused on a lighter topic. "Who is the that for?"

"Gio," Julia said with a smirk.

"Really? I can't picture him wearing it."

"Me either, which is why it'll be a hoot to tell him I think it's sexy."

"You are so bad, Julia," Gigi said with a laugh.

Julia accepted the bag from the vendor with a smile and walked out onto the street with Gigi. "Marriage is work, Gigi, but it's also supposed to be fun. Life is too short and often too sad to take everything so seriously. I'm looking at that castle and thinking about what it must have been like back then. If I were a maiden back then and some knight wanted to win my favor, I would have given him a quest."

"Like slaying a dragon for you?"

Julia's eyes rounded. "Slay? Never. Tame? Yes. Anyone can kill something. I'd want a knight who could bring me a dragon I could ride."

As they approached The Witchery, Gigi spotted Gio near the door of the restaurant with a bouquet of pink roses in his hand. Beside him were several people, holding similar bouquets. "Are all of those for you?"

Julia let out a happy sigh. "Oh, he does know what I love."

Gigi gave Julia a quick hug because she was happy her brother had married such an amazing woman. "Thank you for today, Julia." She glanced around. "I don't see Kane."

Julia hugged her back. "He'll be here, Gigi."

Gigi scanned the area around the restaurant and squared her shoulders when there was no sign of him. She had thrown him out of her place in just a towel that morning. Maybe she deserved to be stood up. Julia stepped away to greet Gio. He gave his wife a tender kiss that brought tears to Gigi's eyes. He didn't care that people stopped and stared because he was in the middle of all those flowers. All Gio cared about was Julia. What would it be like to be loved like that?

Gigi didn't doubt for a second that Gio would tame a dragon for Julia if she ever asked him to. That realization was both beautiful and depressing at the same time. Beautiful because Julia was a warmhearted, kind woman who deserved a man like that.

Depressing because Gigi had never known that kind of love, nor had her mother. Gigi thought how quickly she'd slept with Kane, how little she'd expected from him. *Is Julia right? Did I let myself be swept away by the sex because I don't think I'm worthy of more?*

Kane stepped out of the restaurant, and Gigi's breath caught in her throat. He just kept getting better looking. Immaculately dressed in a dark suit that complemented his broad shoulders well, Gigi knew she wasn't the only woman who found it difficult not to openly stare at the perfection of him. His dark good looks, along with the confident way he held himself, made even a few men stop and wonder who he was.

He smiled at Gigi, and her body went haywire.

So what if he's gorgeous? And smells good. And is phenomenal in bed. One night does not a relationship make. Not even one as good as what we had.

If Gio hadn't arrived, Kane might have already returned to London. Or the States. For all she knew, Kane might consider her a one-night stand, who unfortunately was his best friend's sister. It wasn't as if he'd ever even taken her on a date. Or even asked her out on one.

She forced herself to look away. As far as she could tell, he hadn't brought apology roses either. A few minutes ago Gigi had worried he wouldn't show up, but now that he had, it was no longer enough.

I've never asked a man to tame a dragon for me. Maybe it's time I do.

✧ ✧ ✧

NOTHING MAKES AN empty-handed man look worse than standing beside another man who brought five hundred fucking pink roses. And then to have them handed out to people who walked by? *Thanks Gio. It's going to be a long dinner. Now I get to endure it while feeling like an even bigger ass.*

Julia was already tucked against her husband's side, smiling up at him. Apparently all had been forgiven there. Gigi, on the other hand, was refusing to look at Kane even when he walked over to greet her. He leaned down to kiss her, and she offered him her cheek as if they hadn't just spent the night tasting every inch of each other's bodies. Was she playing it cool because her brother was there, or was she still angry? Kane couldn't tell. He wasn't a man used to being unsure of himself in any situation, but he didn't know how to navigate this one.

He and Gio had come to somewhat of a truce, one that relied on not discussing Gigi. It put Kane in the difficult position of wanting to talk to Gigi alone and respecting a friendship very important to him. They might disagree now and then, but . . .

"Gigi, look at me. Are you okay?" Kane asked softly enough for only her ears to hear.

She looked up at him from beneath her beautifully long lashes, and his heart constricted in his chest. "I wasn't sure you'd come."

He placed a hand lightly on the lower part of her back as he leaned down to say, "Nothing could keep me away. I'm an ass. I told myself to take it slowly with you, but that whole plan went to hell the moment I saw you again. Something happens to my brain when I'm around you."

Gigi raised a hand to caress the side of Kane's face. "I know exactly how that feels."

"Our table is ready," Gio said gruffly. He and Julia led the way through the door, into the reception, and down the stone stairs into the elegant dining area. They were seated in a quiet corner near a window that looked out onto the secluded garden terrace.

Had Gio and Julia not been there, the meal might have been followed by a romp in one of The Witchery's notoriously decadent upstairs suites. Unfortunately, it didn't appear any part of the night before would be repeated that evening.

After ordering drinks, the four of them studied their menus in silence. Kane reached over and took Gigi's hand in his. Gio made an audible displeased sound from behind his menu, proof he was watching them even as he appeared not to be.

Gigi cried out softly and hunched over, pulling her hand away to rub at her leg beneath the table.

Julia blushed, then raised her own menu higher, saying, "Sorry, Gigi, I was aiming for Gio."

Kane choked back a laugh.

Gio lowered his menu. "You think this is funny, Kane?"

Kane lowered his own menu and met his friend's glare calmly. "If by funny, you mean amusing because it's the most painfully awkward dinner I've had the pleasure of being invited to, then yes."

"It'll be fine if you can keep your hands to yourself."

"Then we should make it a quick meal," Kane said only because he was getting tired of apologizing for something he couldn't change. He felt a sudden, sharp kick from Julia beneath the table and winced.

Julia smiled from behind her menu. "Good. My aim is getting better." She closed her menu and leaned toward the two men. "Gigi and I had a fabulous day, and we're about to enjoy what I hope will be an equally amazing dinner in a beautiful magical restaurant. If the two of you want to engage in a male pissing contest, take it somewhere else."

Gio let out a long sigh. He looked back and forth between Gigi and Kane. "I don't like this, but I guess there's nothing I can do about it. If you're not good to my sister, Kane, I'll have your balls on a platter."

A waiter cleared his throat beside the table. "That is not currently one of our specials, but instead may I suggest some Oban native oysters from Argyllshire."

Julia covered her smile. Gigi raised her napkin as she did the same. The look Gio shot the waiter would have caused many powerful men to shake in their shoes, but the waiter was young and quite unimpressed, which only increased Gio's irritation. Kane let out a laugh that couldn't be held in.

"Give us a minute," Gio said to the waiter then turned to his dinner mates. A reluctant smile spread across his face. He raised an eyebrow at Gigi. "You, too?"

Gigi shrugged and lowered her napkin, smiling widely for the first time since they'd entered the restaurant. "You should have seen your face."

With that, the tone of the meal lightened. Gio asked Gigi if she intended to stay in Scotland. Her answer was interrupted by the waiter returning to take their orders, but after he left she continued to describe how she'd fallen in love with the small city. "I love it here. There are so many layers to this city. When I first came here I thought I would easily fit right in. Because of the language, it felt like a quaint version of London to me. But the longer I stayed, the more I realized how very different it is, in a thousand wonderful ways. The joy became seeking out those differences and embracing them. And somehow, over time, it became home to me. Now I can't imagine living anywhere else."

Gigi described how much her friend Annelise had helped her in the beginning and how their friendship had morphed into being business partners, and although Kane had heard the story before, he loved watching Gigi tell it. Part of it, though, gave him an uneasy feeling he had trouble labeling. He hadn't thought much beyond how to get Gigi back in his arms, but hearing her talk about her business and ties in Edinburgh made Kane question something he hadn't considered. He'd assumed if things worked out between them, she would naturally follow him back to New York. What if that wasn't the case?

There was so much he wanted to ask her. In New York he'd focused on his physical attraction to her. He found he also wanted to know what she was thinking, her favorite music, if she liked or hated thunderstorms. Anything and everything about her. He wanted to know it all. "You said you and Annelise are working on a side project right now? What is it?"

Their food was delivered, and Gigi pushed hers around her plate while seeming to debate if she wanted to answer his question. Finally she looked across at Gio and said, "I didn't want to mention it to you, Gio, because I don't want it to be an issue. After Papa died, I asked to go to school in London. My mother paid for a private school by working two jobs and selling off many valuable items from the palazzo. I want to return those items to her."

Kane fell a little bit in love with her just then and took her hand in his again. "I'm sure that means a lot to her."

Gigi raised her eyes to his. "She doesn't know I'm doing it. Which might be for the best, since I'm not doing it well. Some of the items are quite rare, and the collectors who purchased them don't want to part with them. It doesn't matter how much money I offer them."

Julia tapped her hand on the table in inspiration. "Such a shame. Too bad someone can't help you with that."

Gio started to say, "I could—" but stopped when Julia put her hand on his arm and shook her head.

It wasn't very subtle, but Julia wasn't subtle by nature. Her sincere desire for those around her to be happy more than made up for that tiny fault. Kane gave Gigi's hand a squeeze. "I have many contacts in Europe. Some of them might be able to loosen the grip of those collectors."

A hopeful expression lit Gigi's face. "You would do that for me? It's an extensive list."

There were many things Kane wasn't sure about when it came to Gigi, but he was sure if she wanted something as badly as she wanted this, he would move heaven and earth to make it happen for her. "Give me the list and what you know about where each item went, and I'll get them for you."

Gigi's eyes lit up. "Like a quest."

Kane wouldn't have described it that way, but his chest puffed up with pride, nonetheless. "If you want to call it that."

Gigi rose slightly from her chair and gave Kane a grateful kiss, full on his lips. It started chastely, but quickly deepened.

Gio growled audibly.

Kane didn't care. It only took one touch from Gigi to make him forget where he was and who was there. He was on fire for her, just as she instantly became for him. She dug her hands into his hair and held him with the same desperation he felt.

A sharp kick to his shin from Julia brought him back to reality, and he reluctantly broke off the kiss. He and Gigi sat back and let out matching, shaky sighs. They exchanged a guilty, passion-filled glance before attempting to return their attention to the others.

Julia said cheerfully, "The food here is amazing, but I'm getting tired. Let's see if we can get that check."

Chapter Seventeen

After dinner, Gigi and Kane walked hand in hand farther up The Royal Mile to the castle at the top. The courtyard was still open even though the castle grounds were closed. Kane sat on a cement wall overlooking Edinburgh and pulled Gigi forward between his legs. The air was charged with their attraction to each other. Gigi was one touch away from mauling Kane publicly like a randy teenager. He took both of her hands in his and gave her a lusty smile, apparently having similar thoughts.

"Your apartment was wonderful, but my hotel is closer," he murmured against her neck in a bedroom voice that filled Gigi's mind with stimulating memories of how they'd spent the night before. The evidence of his urgency was pressed deliciously against her abdomen.

The memory of how he'd felt in her hand, her mouth, deep inside her, had her quivering with need. Her body craved his. All she had to do was say yes and the pleasure from the night before would be hers again. Maybe it was the castle beside them, or Julia's earlier observation that Gigi deserved better than she asked for, but Gigi wanted more than hot sex with a man who may or may not have feelings for her. The maiden Julia had referenced wouldn't have asked her knight in shining armor to tame a dragon, only to sleep with him as soon as he agreed to. No, she would have waited for his victorious return.

Gigi pulled back slightly from Kane, still holding his hands, but breaking all other contact. "I don't want to sleep with you again. Not yet."

For a moment Kane looked so shocked it was almost comical. "Last night was amazing for me. You didn't feel the same way?"

Gigi blushed. "It was incredible."

"But?"

Unable to look him in the eye while trying to express herself, Gigi kept her eyes focused on the top button of his shirt. "My mother spent half of her life with a man who wouldn't leave his wife for her."

"I'm not married," Kane said.

Gigi gave his hands a squeeze and looked up. "Hear me out."

Kane opened his mouth as if to say something, then closed it and nodded.

"My father said he loved us, but he could only love us so much, you know? He had another family who needed him. I didn't realize how much it had affected me until recently. I've kept my expectations of people very low so they won't disappoint me. I think that's wrong. I don't want half of anyone."

A storm raged in Kane's eyes. "I don't know what to say,

Gigi."

Emotion brought tears to Gigi's eyes, but they weren't from sadness. At least, not about what Kane was saying. They were tears of growth as Gigi faced a part of herself she'd denied. "I know, Kane. What can you say? We've really only had one night together. But that's my point. We did this—us—backward. I know how I feel around you. I know how tempting it is to give in to that feeling, but I need more than that."

Kane let out a long breath and looked away for a moment then back. "What do you want, Gigi?"

Gigi looked deeply into his eyes and spoke from her heart. "Everything—or nothing. If that's not what you're looking for, let's end this now. You offered to help me find my mother's things, but I'll understand if you don't want to do that anymore. I don't regret last night, but it can't happen again, not yet."

Kane's face was tight with emotion. Gigi wasn't sure what he was thinking. She moved to disentangle her hands from his, but he held her firmly before him. "I promised to get your mother's items back to you and I will, but only on one condition . . ."

Gigi held his eyes and swallowed hard. For a brief second she worried he would make her an offer that would change how she felt about him. Could she blame him if he did? She'd slept with him so quickly he might think the worst of her. She fought back the insecurities begging to surface. Insecurities tied to having a mother who had been someone's mistress. Would that be his offer?

Kane brought one of her hands to his lips. "I want you to come with me when I negotiate for the items. We'll get them back for your mother, but we'll get them back together."

Panic brought a shake to Gigi's hands. "You understand I don't want to—"

Kane kissed the inside of her wrist. "I got that."

Gigi scanned his face for a clue of how he felt about it. "And you're okay with it?"

Kane pulled her back against him, looping his hands behind her waist. His arousal was still proudly prominent in his trousers, the feel of it against her almost made Gigi change her mind. She licked her bottom lip and fought against the desire growing within her.

When he spoke, his voice was deep and sure. "It'll be torture to be around you and not take you where we've been, but if waiting is important to you, then it's important to me."

Fresh tears spilled down Gigi's cheeks. She grabbed his face between her hands and kissed him soundly. He returned the kiss, but instead of deepening it, he ended it by lifting his head with a groan. "Go easy on the gratitude, though. I'm only human."

✧ ✧ ✧

KANE HAD SPENT the last three weeks traveling back and forth between Edinburgh and London. His plan for additional headquarters was still very much up in the air but only because he was now looking into Scotland's viability as a location. He didn't want to admit yet that it had anything to do with Gigi, but he didn't think he was fooling anyone.

Although he hadn't said anything to Gigi yet, he'd also spent an hour or so each day tracking down the items on the list Gigi had given him. If the request to purchase an item was easily granted, he completed the transaction and had it shipped to a storage facility he'd rented near Venice. If the collector requested to meet him in person, he sent the information to Marge in New York so she could adjust the flight schedule and lodging for what was growing into a several-week agenda.

When he'd first informed Marge of the trip, he'd told her he was helping Gio's family with a project. He'd revealed more than he'd meant to when he asked Marge to make sure the lodging she chose for each stop was both efficiently located and romantic.

Marge had sputtered in surprise. "Romantic? Are you taking Gigi with you?"

Part of him had wanted to tell her it was none of her business, but since she was making the arrangements for the trip—it was essential for her to know who to plan for. He'd said, "I sure hope so."

As if the news hadn't shocked her at all, she'd calmly clarified, "One room or two?"

He'd sighed, "Two."

"Oh," she'd said. "Don't worry, it'll all work out. May I say something on a personal note?"

"No."

That didn't stop Marge. *Of course.* "You're doing this the right way. Your friendship with Gio is too important to rush into something that could jeopardize that. Plus, you're old enough to understand that it's time for you to stop hopping from one woman to the next. This is good for you."

Her words had rung too close to the opinion of someone else Kane knew. "Have you been talking to my mother?"

Marge had laughed. "She was here yesterday with your father. He looks so happy to be in the office again. Your mother said he could play here until you give them grandchildren and then spoiling them will be his only occupation."

"Goodbye, Marge." Kane had hung up with a pained chuckle. Coming from a close family had benefits *and* drawbacks.

Time had flown by. He'd had dinner with Gigi several nights a week. They'd stayed as far away from her apartment and his hotel as they could. It was frustrating, but surprisingly satisfying in a way. He couldn't remember the last time he had eagerly anticipated anything as much as he did seeing her each evening. They had an unexpected number of things in common, and one of those was an appreciation of Edinburgh.

At first, it had been nothing more than a small city to Kane, one that just happened to be where Gigi lived. However, the friendly nature of its people was winning him over. He and Gigi often nursed a drink at one of the local pubs while swapping stories about their lives. They discovered they both found the stare of housecats unnerving. Although they liked different music, they laughed at the same comedians. When they compared their bucket lists, there were several items they had in common. Their age difference didn't matter now that Gigi was older.

They did find one subject they disagreed on. They'd been sitting in a pub listening to a local band when Kane had asked Gigi to say something to him in Italian, and she had refused. She'd claimed not to speak it anymore even though he had heard her use it quite fluently at her brothers' weddings. He thought back to when he'd visited her mother's house and remembered that she'd spoken, even then, only in English.

"Aren't you Venetian?" Kane had asked because he'd wanted to gauge her reaction to the question.

"My mother is," Gigi had answered stiffly, pulling back from him emotionally. He could almost see her slamming up protective walls to hide behind.

He'd kept his tone light. "So, what do you consider yourself?"

"Not my mother," Gigi had answered shortly. "Can we talk about something else?"

Kane had let the topic drop, but it had reminded him of something her mother had said. Leora had lost more than her lover and her paintings; she had lost her daughter as well. He hoped to rectify that one day.

Kane was walking to meet Gigi for dinner when his phone rang. Nick. "Hello."

"Kane, I'm in Edinburgh with Luke and Max. We need to see you. Tonight."

"What the hell are you doing here?"

"We'll tell you when we see you. Come to the hotel."

"I can't right this minute. I'm meeting Gigi."

"Gigi's fine. She's with Rena and the girls."

Kane stopped dead in his tracks. "Did something happen?"

"Meet us in the bar on the first floor." With that, Nick hung up.

Kane hailed a taxi. A variety of horrible possibilities played out in his mind. He called Gio.

"Hello?" Gio answered curtly.

"Thank God. I thought you were dead."

"That's a novel way of saying you missed me."

"Hey, Nick just called me. He's here in Edinburgh with Max and Luke. They want to talk to me."

"And you thought that meant I had kicked the bucket?"

"The possibility had crossed my mind. They said Gigi is with their wives. It sounded serious."

"It was. Gigi called Julia, and she was upset."

"Upset? I've been with Gigi every day. If she were upset I'd know about it. What did she tell Julia?"

"I don't know. Julia wouldn't tell me."

"Why are your brothers all here?"

"I promised Gigi I wouldn't get involved."

"So you sent them?"

"I am not my brothers' keeper. I can't stop them from going over there and beating the shit out of you if you've done something to hurt Gigi."

"I haven't hurt Gigi. We're dating. That's it."

"Save your explanations for my brothers." Gio hung up.

Kane started swearing. He tapped the window between

him and the cab driver and gave him new instructions. He had no problem meeting up with Nick and the others, but he had something he had to do first.

Before he answered anyone else's questions, he had a few of his own—questions only Gigi could answer.

Chapter Eighteen

FEELING A LITTLE shell-shocked, Gigi followed a waiter to a table and took a seat with three of her sisters-in-law. She smiled at each of them tentatively. She was still new to having a large family. Was this what they did? Descend en masse without warning? She didn't hate the idea, but it definitely wasn't what she was used to. "What a nice surprise. Kane should be here any minute."

Rena looked at Cassie and Tara before saying, "I wouldn't count on him showing up for a little while."

Gigi's stomach did a nervous flip. "Did something happen?"

"Not yet," Rena said mysteriously.

Luke's wife, Cassie, put her hand near Gigi's on the table. "We're all here to make sure you're okay."

Gigi studied each of the women's faces again. Tara, Max's wife, nodded in agreement. "Why wouldn't I be?"

Rena tapped a finger thoughtfully on the edge of her plate. "I told Nick we should call you, but when Gio gets worked up about something, the family charges first and asks questions later."

"I don't understand," Gigi said slowly, then remembered something. "What did Julia say?"

Tara looked to Cassie. "I don't know. Do you?"

Cassie looked to Rena.

Rena shrugged. "Nick didn't give me specifics. He said Gio called him and said he needed to find out what Kane had done to upset you."

Cassie added, "Nick called Luke for his opinion?"

Tara waved a hand in the air in conclusion. "Luke called Max and voila, here we are. Are you saying that Kane didn't do anything?"

Gigi covered her face with her hands for a moment. "This is bad. This isn't what I wanted at all." She lowered her hands and quickly met the eyes of each woman. "I'd explain, but it's a long story."

A waitress came by and took drink orders. Once she left, Rena said, "We have time. Start at the beginning."

Gigi went beet-red as she remembered how she and Kane had spent their first night. Cassie rushed to assure her, "Or whatever part you're comfortable sharing."

Gigi shook her head. "You will all think I'm . . ."

Rena sat back in her chair and said, "Gigi, whatever is going on, we've all been there. I hid my relationship with Nick for a long time then almost lost him because I was too afraid to trust what we had."

Tara chimed in. "There was a point when I thought Max and I wouldn't work out. Every relationship has its challenges."

Cassie took a sip of her water and then added, "Right up

until Luke proposed I wasn't sure what was happening between us. So, trust us, Gigi, whatever you say isn't going to shock us."

Gigi chewed her lip for a moment as she debated how much to share. When she started talking, it all spilled out. Every last bit of it. She told them how she'd met Kane first at their wedding, how he'd been when he'd come to Venice. She looked away and said they may have rushed into things when Kane first came to Scotland. "I called Julia because I'm so confused. I asked Kane to take things slowly, and he has. He's been wonderful. In some ways I feel like we started over, built a friendship where there had only been a physical attraction before. We've spent a lot of time together, but now he's dropping me off at my place without even trying to come in. I'm starting to worry. Did I suck the life out of something by trying to make it into what it wasn't? I don't want to be his friend. I want more. But what if I've ruined it? I called Julia because I needed to get it out of my head. I told her I was thinking about breaking up with Kane."

Tara waved frantically at Gigi, but Gigi was finishing off her thought and didn't stop.

"So, you see, Kane is not the problem. It's me. I don't want to be with him like this."

Rena place one hand on Gigi's arm and pointed above her shoulder with her other. Gigi cringed and turned slowly. "Kane."

There was a definite hardness in his expression that Gigi had never seen before. He looked as if he were about to say something, then turned on his heel and strode out of the dining room.

Gigi turned to the other women in horror. "How much did he hear?"

Rena whistled. "I'd say only the worst part."

Tara threw her napkin on the table. "What are you waiting for? Go after him."

Gigi hesitated.

Cassie looked on sympathetically. "Unless you really don't want to be with him."

Gigi stood. She knew why she had issues trusting men. Deep inside the strong woman she considered herself to be, there was still a young girl who had believed her father would never leave her, a girl who had never gotten over the way he'd left her. She hated how hard it made her to believe in anyone.

Gigi thought about how sweet Kane had been to her for the last month. She didn't chase him because she didn't know what she'd say if she caught him. There was one more piece to how Gigi was feeling that she hadn't told the other women about. She didn't want to face it herself.

Kane, it's worse than what you heard. Much more fucked up than that.

I'm falling in love with you.

And I'm terrified.

I'm afraid to lose you.

But I'm more afraid I'll change to keep you.

You've done nothing to find my mother's belongings, but I want you so much, I tell myself it doesn't matter. I'll take you on your terms.

I'm ready to beg you to stay with me, no matter what that means.

That's how my mother was with my father, and I hate myself for feeling this way.

Oh, Kane. Why couldn't you have at least tried to bring me a dragon?

Rena touched Gigi's arm softly. "Are you okay?"

Gigi shook her head and rubbed her forehead with a shaky hand. "No. No, I don't think I am."

She excused herself and stepped outside the restaurant. She called the one person who knew her better than anyone else. Annelise. She felt badly about walking away from her family, but they were still getting to know her. She needed someone who knew both her and Kane. Annelise had seen them together many times over the last few weeks. And she understood Gigi's reluctance to trust men. She'd be able to unravel the tangle Gigi's thoughts were in.

A few hours and two bottles of wine later, Annelise tucked herself beneath a throw blanket on Gigi's couch. "Do you want my opinion?"

Gigi took one last gulp of wine and tucked her bare feet up beneath her on the chair across from her friend. "That's why I called you."

"I like Kane."

"But?"

"But you're not ready for him."

Alcohol put a slur to Gigi's next words. "Technically, I've already been with him."

"That's not what I mean. Some people are like racecars.

Zero to love with no looking back. That has never been you. Hell, how long did you avoid your brothers before finally meeting with them?"

Gigi leaned her head back and closed her eyes. "I'm a coward."

"Maybe not a coward, but you have some serious trust issues."

Gigi opened one eye. "Thanks, Annelise. You're not making me feel better."

Annelise shrugged. "You didn't call me because you wanted me to cheer you up. You asked me what I thought, so here it is. You push people away then you wonder why they leave. You say you do it because you're scared. Okay. We all get scared. We've all been disappointed by someone. My question is: What are you going to do about it?"

"Do? About Kane?"

"I don't care about Kane. Kane is irrelevant. I'm talking about you. What are you going to do to conquer that fear? Until you do, you'll never trust anyone because you can't trust yourself."

Ouch. The truth was painful. Gigi put her glass of wine down with a sense of finality. "Can you cover the office for a few days? There is someone I need to talk to."

Annelise nodded and yawned, before closing her eyes and saying, "Tell your mother I said hello."

✧ ✧ ✧

Kane downed a shot of Dalwhinnie Scotch in the bar of his hotel. He waved for the bartender to bring him another.

He was D.O.N.E. Done.

With Scotland. With Gigi. With love.

If he'd doubted his feelings before hearing Gigi say she wanted to break up with him, the pain spreading through his gut to all of his extremities confirmed it. Nothing but love could cut a man so deeply.

He'd briefly considered confronting Gigi at the restaurant, but short of throwing her over his shoulder, carrying her out of the restaurant, and demanding she love him, there wasn't much he could say. Especially not beneath the watchful eyes of the Andrade wives. No, it hadn't been the time or the place to address what she'd said.

The irony of it was he'd done everything Gigi had asked. He'd played by her rules, waited because she'd asked him to. His desire for her had burned like an eternal torch within him, but it hadn't been unbearable. He found pleasure in her laughter, in the way she wrinkled her nose at him when she disagreed with something he said, and in the simple warmth of her hand in his.

He'd never met a woman who could make him feel giddy with just a look. When she complimented him, he felt invincible. There was not one part of their month together that hadn't felt significant. Each time he saw her he fell a little more in love with her.

He had begun to see forever in her eyes while *she'd* been planning her exit strategy. How could he not have known she was that unhappy? He scoured every memory he had of them together. What did Gigi want that he hadn't given her?

A month of putting his own needs aside for hers surfaced

as irritation and frustration. He downed his second shot. *This is what happens when you date someone you know you shouldn't. I saw this coming. I told myself to steer clear. But I went for it anyway.*

Out of the corner of his eye he noted the seats on either side of him filled simultaneously. He tensed and briefly glanced in one direction and then the other.

Luke Andrade was on his right. Nick and Max were on his left.

Perfect.

Kane waved down the bartender for a refill. "I'm in no mood to talk."

Nick pushed a hundred-pound bill across to the bartender and motioned with a move to his neck for Kane to be cut off.

Kane put two hundred on the bar and motioned for another. "Keep 'em coming."

Nick slapped another hundred down and handed all four to the bartender then waved him away. He put a hand on Kane's shoulder. "There is nothing good at the bottom of a bottle."

Kane shrugged his hand off. "Don't fucking touch me."

Nick raised his hands in mock surrender and said lightly, "Hey, I'm on your side."

From the other side of Nick, Max said, "He is. He actually wanted to come find you. I'm here under some coercion. Don't get me wrong, I hope you and Gigi work it all out, but I don't want to know the details."

Luke pushed a glass of water in front of Kane. "Real nice,

Max. Kane, bottling your feelings up isn't healthy. Cassie told me what happened at the restaurant."

Kane picked up the glass of water and rolled it, swirling the water within. "I don't want to discuss it."

"Cassie said Gigi was describing how she'd called Julia because she was considering breaking it off with you. She wasn't saying she was still going to."

Nick interjected, "I don't see how that is any better."

Luke countered, "I'm trying to make a point, Nick. Kane only heard part of the conversation."

Pushing the water away, Kane said angrily, "I heard enough."

"Gigi cares about you," Luke stressed.

"Really?" Kane asked harshly. "I would have believed that yesterday. Today, I'm not sure about anything."

Nick drummed his fingers on the table. "Me, either. Rena tried to explain it to me, but all I got out of it was you're not an asshole, and Gigi is confused."

"Are we done?" Kane asked abruptly.

"Not yet," Luke said, laying one hand flat on the wooden bar beside him. "Do you love Gigi?"

Kane shoved the water away from him and growled, "I'd be a fool if I did."

"You didn't answer the question."

"What do you want, Luke? You want me to say until about an hour ago I thought Gigi and I had a future together? Do you want me to describe how hearing her say she wanted to break it off with me felt like someone stabbing me with a dull knife? That I can't think straight yet because I still don't believe she didn't enjoy this past month as much as I did?"

Max leaned into the conversation. "Oh, man, you do have it bad for her."

Kane slapped his hand on the bar and stood. "Thanks for checking in on me, but this conversation is over."

Luke surprised Kane by stepping in front of him, blocking his exit. Had it been either of the other men, Kane would have given them a not-so-subtle shove out of his way. But getting aggressive with Luke would feel like swearing at Gandhi. In a low, tight voice, Kane said, "Get out of my way."

Luke took out his phone, dialed a number, then held it up between them and put the call on speakerphone. "Gio? Yeah, we found him. He's taking it pretty hard."

"He should. His ass needs to be over there apologizing," Gio said shortly.

Kane snorted angrily. "For what exactly?"

Gio didn't have a ready response to that, so instead he said, "For possibly ruining everything. We finally have Gigi in our lives. I won't lose her over something like this."

"How she feels or doesn't feel about me has nothing to do with her relationship with you."

"You're wrong. This is exactly what I didn't want to happen. If you two break up, she'll want to avoid you, and that means avoiding us."

Kane shrugged. "Then I'll make sure I'm not around."

Gio barked, "No one wants that either."

Max interjected, "Fifty pounds on him saying it."

Nick shook his head, "You're on. He won't. He's too angry."

Kane hunched his shoulders. "I'm sorry, Gio. I knew it was a bad idea to come here, but I couldn't stop myself."

"Kane, people make mistakes, and you're like family to us. If being perfect was a requirement for that, do you think the three little shits next to you would still be around?"

"Hey." Max laughed as he pretended to be offended. "He's referring to us, Nick."

"That's because he's angry, not deaf," Luke said dryly.

Nick joked, "For the record, Gio, the bet was Max's idea."

"Way to throw me under the bus," Max countered and gave Nick's shoulder a shove. "Besides, Luke, Gio said three. You would be one of those little shits he's referring to."

A hint of a smile pulled at Kane's lips as he watched the men bicker. He'd known them since they were all in their early teens. Although they had each become successful, they sounded remarkably the same as they had back then. "I get your point, Gio, but I'm not apologizing when I have no idea what I'm supposed to have done wrong."

Nick added, "In my experience, if you give a woman a chance to, she'll tell you. Several times, until she's sure you get it."

Max joked, "Rena must have the patience of a saint."

Nick stood taller. "Don't talk about my wife unless you want yours to know about the year you kept wetting your bed."

"Enough," Luke said curtly and turned off the speakerphone and put his phone back near his ear. "To me, this is something Kane and Gigi have to work out for themselves." After a pause, Luke said, "I agree. Yes, I'll tell him."

After hanging up the phone, Luke turned to Kane. "Gio said he's relieved you didn't do something we'd have to hurt you for. He also told me to tell you he loves you."

"Ha," Max said triumphantly. "Fifty pounds, Nick. I told you."

Nick looked at Luke skeptically. "Did he actually say it?"

Luke shrugged one shoulder shamelessly. "No, I'm just screwing with you. He did agree we should pull back and let Kane and Gigi figure this out."

Luke the Pacifier had blatantly poked fun at his brothers. Kane didn't hide his surprise.

An easy smile spread across Luke's face. "I'm not perfect, and I embrace that fact now. I can't let them have all the fun."

Although it was nice to see Luke joking with his brothers instead of having to play the peacekeeper, Kane grumbled and turned back to the bar. His mood was still sour. "If you don't mind, I came here with a goal that you've delayed." Luke sat on the stool beside him. Nick and Max retook the seats on his other side. Kane took in the stubborn expressions on the men who flanked him, and an entirely different feeling swept through him. Luke, Nick, and Max might have flown over to confront him, but they were staying because they cared about him.

Kane ordered four sodas and toasted the Andrade men around him.

When they raised their glasses, too, Max said, "To family."

They all drank to that.

In the long silence that followed, Kane admitted to himself he would apologize to Gigi a hundred times if it would help. It wouldn't. She wasn't angry with him. She didn't know if she wanted to be with him anymore. That wasn't an issue an apology would solve.

Kane thought about his father's favorite speech about why everyone should play a sport when they're young. His father had said, "Life is going to knock you down sometimes. You need to know what to do when it happens. When you land on your ass, you don't give up and go home. You stand back up and try harder. Surrender is not an option. Not in sports. Not in life."

It was a philosophy that had served Kane well during his athletic years, as well as in business. When he set a goal he went after it relentlessly, again and again, until he achieved it. Failure was not in his vocabulary.

This was different. If winning meant Gigi or her family lost in some way, it wasn't something he would pursue. He couldn't do that to Gio or his brothers any more than he could do it to the woman he loved.

He closed his eyes and pinched the bridge of his nose. More than anything else, he wanted Gigi to be happy. Plain and simple. Her childhood had been full of confusion and doubt. Although she had reunited with her father's side of the family, it was still a fragile bond, and Gio was right to protect it.

Pursuing Gigi was not an option. Even the heaven of spending another night in her arms was not worth the collateral damage it might cause.

I knew that before I came here, and it didn't stop me, but the only deplorable mistakes are those a person makes twice.

As she frequently did in person, his mother followed his father's life advice with some of her own. It might have been the alcohol rushing through his system, but he could hear her as clearly as if she were there. "No one wins every time, Kane. Not even your father. When you do lose, accept it and grow from it. There is good in even the darkest of days. If you look for it and don't find it, make it."

Kane opened his eyes and broke the silence. "I've been working on something for Gigi. It's a project that needs to be completed even if she and I are no longer together."

Kane shared that Leora had asked him to help Gigi find her way back to her Venetian roots. He explained how Gigi's mother had sold off her belongings to pay for her daughter's schooling, and how Gigi had been determined to repurchase everything she'd sold.

"Why wouldn't she ask for our help?" Nick asked.

With a sympathetic expression on his face, Luke said, "She might not feel she can yet."

Max shook his head in confusion. "We're her brothers. We'd do anything for her."

In a low voice, Kane said, "If she doesn't rely on you, you can't disappoint her again."

All four men fell into a pensive quiet.

Taking a last swig of his soda, Kane said, "I have most of

the items already. They're stored just outside of Venice. I had planned to bring Gigi with me while I negotiated for the remaining items. I'll complete those purchases this week and have everything in that storage facility. All you need to do is take Gigi there, and she'll handle the rest."

Luke turned in his chair to face Kane and his brothers. "Does she know you're doing this?"

"When she first mentioned some of the collectors were holding tight to some of the paintings, I offered to help her. I didn't tell her I had started the project. I'd planned to surprise her."

Nick looked skyward. "Oh, boy."

Max whistled. "Even I can see the problem with this one. Gigi doesn't handle surprises well."

"Most of it was hardly a surprise. She's the one who gave me the list of each item."

"Interesting," Luke said slowly as if he were fitting pieces of a puzzle together.

Nick shook his head. "He doesn't get it."

Luke began drumming his fingers on the bar again. "It would explain why she's so upset. I bet she thinks you haven't done anything to get those items back."

Kane snapped around to meet Luke's eyes. Could it be that simple? "She never asked about it."

Luke shrugged one shoulder. "As you said, you can't disappoint her if she doesn't rely on you."

Kane fisted his hand on the table. "I would do anything for her. She has to know that."

Max interjected, "So are we all going to sit here and

commiserate on being the people she has no faith in, or are we going to do something about it?"

"Do something?" Nick parroted.

Luke sighed. "Trust isn't something you can force, Max."

"Maybe not," Max replied, "but you can damn well prove yourself worthy of it." He turned to Kane. "Before we do this, I need to know if you love Gigi. I mean, the forever after type of love. Because if we do this right, you just might end up married to her."

Chapter Nineteen

Gigi sat on a stool in her mother's kitchen in Venice and watched her mother rolling pasta. "We need to talk, Mamma."

Leora paused and glanced at Gigi. "I figured as much. You don't usually come home without a good reason."

Gigi rubbed her cold hands on the thighs of her slacks and blurted, "Why did you accept that Papa wouldn't leave his wife? Why didn't you ever demand more from him? Didn't you think we deserved better than he gave us?"

Leora stopped and wiped her hands on a towel. "I loved him, Gigia. And he left you as much money as he did his sons. That must mean something to you."

Gigi stood angrily. "Yes, he gave me money, and he gave you this palazzo, but if he had actually loved either of us, he would have left his wife. He wouldn't have kept us hidden. You were nothing but his mistress, and I was his bastard child."

"That's enough, Gigia. Your father is not here to defend himself, and I will not allow you to speak badly of him. He was a good man."

"Do you know how many times I've heard you describe him that way? But you're wrong. He wasn't. Not by my definition. He was a cheater and a liar. Considering the way he hid us from everyone, I would say he was also a coward."

Leora studied Gigi's face for a long moment. "He's gone. He can't change the past. He can't even try to make amends. What are you looking for me to say? Do you want me to hate him with you? I can't. I loved him. I still love him." Gigi frowned and her mother continued, "Are you angry, Gigia, or afraid? I can't help you fight your demons if you don't tell me what they are."

"My demons? Mine? What kind of mother lets her daughter be raised by a man who doesn't love her? A man who fills her head so full of lies she can't believe anyone? What am I afraid of? I'm falling in love with a man, Mamma, and I am terrified I'll end up like you."

Gigi's words hung heavy in the air between them. Although voicing her fears to her mother had been cathartic, the pain in Leora's eyes instantly filled Gigi with remorse. "Mamma—"

Leora raised her hand in a signal for her daughter to stop talking. She raised her chin, sniffed, and dabbed at the corner of one of her eyes. Finally, in a calm voice that was not reflected in her stormy dark eyes, Leora said, "Is that why you wanted to go to school in England? Why you turn your back on your own heritage? Because you're afraid of becoming me?"

Gigi could have lied. It would have been kinder, but she had spent a lifetime concealing how she felt. So, instead, she whispered, "Yes."

Leora rubbed one hand lightly across her face. "You think I stayed with your father because I was too weak to leave him? That I should have been more than some man's mistress?"

Gigi swallowed hard and held her mother's eyes. "Yes."

Pursing her lips, Leora took a moment to choose her words. "You may be right, Gigia. But from the first moment I met your father, I knew we belonged together. He never lied to me. He had given his heart and his name to a woman who could not love him back. They had four sons, and for that reason he would never leave her. He gave me a choice, and I chose him, even though I knew I could never have all of him. He loved me as deeply as he could, and there was not a day together where he wasn't a kind and gentle man. He cried the day you were born because he loved you so very much."

"So much that he never told his other family about me."

Leora clasped her hands in front of her. "You know he did that to protect you."

Gigi shrugged doubtfully. "That's what you've always said."

"His wife was an angry and spiteful woman. You were safer if she didn't know about you."

Gigi looked at the floor. "That sounds like a lie a man tells his mistress to keep her quiet. Papa couldn't very well call his wife a saint because then his unfaithfulness wouldn't have been so easy to excuse."

"Gigia, you're not a child anymore. It's time for you to

stop being angry with your father. And with me. Perhaps I didn't live the life you would have chosen, but I was happy in it. You never went to bed hungry or scared. I made sure you had not only what you needed, but also what your heart was set on. There is nothing I can do or say that will change what you think of me, or how you feel about being Venetian. The only one who can do that is you. I have seen the destructive nature of anger that is allowed to fester within a person's heart. You don't want that. Ask your brothers about their mother. See if holding onto the past is truly what you want to do."

"I don't understand."

"And you won't until you learn that love is not all roses and poems. It's beautifully, painfully more complex than that. And love cannot take root in a heart full of anger. I don't regret a single day I spent with your father. I hope you can one day say the same about whoever you choose."

With that her mother returned to rolling pasta. Gigi asked Leora about adding oregano to the sauce on the stove and they discussed the recipe she was making as if they hadn't just gone into and come out of the most honest conversation they'd ever had.

✧ ✧ ✧

"What do you think of this stone?" Kane asked as he held up a four-carat, flawless brilliant cut diamond for his father to inspect.

His father studied it through a jeweler's loupe. "It's beautiful, even if it's a bit premature. Shouldn't you wait until you and Gigi are back together before you buy an engagement ring?"

"You're the one who says the only good plan is the one you prepare for."

"Yes," his father admitted wryly. "But I don't know if it's possible to plan when it comes to matters of the heart."

"What's the worst thing that happens? She never sees it. Nick made a good point. I should have it if I need it."

Thom's eyes widened as he held the diamond out to Kane. "Nick Andrade? He's giving you relationship advice now?"

Kane paused mid-retrieval. "Said like that, it sounds bad. He's come a long way, Dad."

His father made an amused grimace. "You know I've always considered the Andrade boys to be my other sons. And Nick actually is one now. He and Rena are perfect for each other, but are you sure he's qualified to guide you when it comes to relationships?"

Kane picked up another diamond to inspect. "Three years ago I would have said no, but Nick wants Gigi to be happy as much as I do. We're planning an event that will show Gigi how much they care about her and possibly open the door for me to present this." Kane held up the stone in the diamond tweezers. "We're calling it Operation Trust."

"How does Gio feel about this?"

"You know how he is."

"You haven't told him."

"I will, Dad, but not yet. Our plan has a lot of variables, and Gio wouldn't handle that well. It's better to tell him once we have the details cemented."

His father sat back and folded his arms across his chest. "So, you're secretly planning for a way to win Gigi's trust?"

"Exactly."

"You don't see the irony of that?"

"Dad, I love Gigi. This was the only acceptable way I could show her. Who knew that getting a woman to marry you was a hundred times more complicated than getting her to sleep with you?"

His father opened his mouth to say something, then shut it with a snap. "Will you promise me something?"

"I'll take this one," Kane told the jeweler who had been perfectly still, seemingly trying to blend into the background. "Have your designer call me. This ring needs to be perfect." Kane turned to his father. "Anything, Dad. You know that."

"Run this whole plan by your mother before you go forward with it. She may have suggestions on how to tweak it."

"I think we have everything covered, but it's not a bad idea to get a woman's perspective from someone I trust." Kane stood and stretched. "I've got to get back to the office now. How are you handling being retired again?"

"Good. I don't imagine it will last, though. Sounds like you'll be preoccupied very soon."

Kane smiled widely. "I hope so, Dad. I really hope so."

Chapter Twenty

"Are we there yet?" Annelise joked from her place beside Gigi in the chauffeured sedan.

"Not yet," Gigi said lightly.

"How about now?"

"No."

"Now?"

Gigi chuckled and threw a napkin at Annelise. "Will you stop? I'm wound up enough without you pushing me over the edge."

Annelise opened her purse, took out a compact, and checked her makeup. "I don't see why you're nervous. You've met your uncles before."

Gigi folded her hands on her lap and hoped she looked more confident than she felt. "Yes, but we didn't say much. Kiss. Kiss. Nice to meet you. Glad you're here. That kind of thing."

"But today we're going to rough them up until they tell us what you want to know?"

Gigi chuckled, then sobered and looked out the car window. "I didn't know it was possible to admire someone and still be ashamed of them. I feel like the worst daughter on the planet. I tell myself it's not my place to judge my mother's decisions. I remind myself how much she's done for me, and I want to be okay with what she did, who she chose to be with. But as soon as I started to get serious about Kane, I felt this wall go up inside me. I'd rather be alone, than become my mother. My mother says I'll never be happy while I'm holding on to my anger. And she's right. More than anything, I want to put it aside, but I don't know how. I'm hoping my uncles know something that will help."

Annelise reached out and took one of Gigi's hands in hers. "That's a lot of pressure to put on one conversation."

Gigi met her friend's eyes. "Don't make me start second guessing myself. I'm already asking myself if this is a good idea. I'm getting along with my brothers. I'm reasonably well adjusted. Things aren't great, but they're good enough. Maybe I should leave it at that."

Giving Gigi's hand a supportive squeeze, Annelise said, "We've come too far to chicken out now. You need to stop thinking you're the little girl this family didn't know existed. When you talk to your uncles, be the strong, independent woman I started a business with. When you set your mind to something, you make it happen. This is no different. If you want answers, don't leave until you get them."

Gigi nodded. "You're right. Although lately I've begun to doubt even the business side of myself. Did I tell you I contacted six places I'd heard had my mother's items and not one of them would negotiate a price with me? Four said they had already sold them but wouldn't disclose to whom. And the remaining two wouldn't answer my calls. I'm zero for ten, and it's becoming discouraging. You'd think having money would open doors for me, but it hasn't."

Their car slowed at a large gate, then pulled through and up a long driveway. An impressive mansion sat atop a small hill in the middle of acres of manicured grass. There was more than one gym set. Children's toy vehicles were scattered around the lawn. The door of the home flew open as the car came to a stop at the bottom of the stone steps.

Still tall and well built for his age, Alessandro rushed down the stairs to open the door for Gigi. His petite auburn-haired wife, Elise, was smiling as she followed him.

As soon as Gigi stepped out of the car, she was swept from her feet into a bone-crushing hug. Her uncle swung her around as if she were a child.

"Gigi, your phone call made my day. I can't tell you how happy hearing from you makes me."

From beside him, Elise said, "Alessandro, put poor Gigi down. She's still getting to know us."

He did, and Gigi adjusted her clothing, saying politely, "It's okay. I'm happy to see you, too, Uncle Alessandro." She stepped forward and gave Elise a kiss on the cheek. "You, too, Aunt Elise. Your home is beautiful."

Gigi turned around to introduce Annelise and laughed when she saw that Alessandro was giving her an equally boisterous greeting. "Annelise, meet Uncle Alessandro. Uncle Alessandro, this is my best friend in the whole world, Annelise Douglas."

Alessandro set Annelise back onto her feet and brought

his wife closer to meet her. "We've heard a lot about you, Annelise."

Still laughing from being swung around, Annelise asked, "You have?"

Elise offered her hand to Gigi's friend. "You've been the topic of dinner conversations. Everyone who has met you adores you. Thank you for being so good to our Gigi."

From beside her, Alessandro added, "Just hug them both, Elise. You know you want to."

Elise looked at her husband and then back at Gigi and Annelise. "He's right. I do, but I know it takes time to be comfortable around new people, even if they're related to you."

There was such warmth emanating from her aunt and uncle that Gigi gave in to an impulse. She wrapped her arms around her aunt and gave her a long, tight hug.

When Gigi released her, Annelise did the same then joked, "I'm not even a hugger normally."

Elise wiped happy tears from around her eyes. "I'm sorry, it's just so good to have you here. We've waited so long." She collected herself and started up the steps. "Come, you didn't come all this way to spend the day in the driveway. We have a wonderful brunch planned. Richard is cooking today. He's making my grandmother's sauce with Alessandro's mother's meatballs. And a fruit crostata for dessert. You'll each go home five pounds heavier, but it's heaven."

In a slight panic, Annelise whispered to Gigi, "I didn't know we were eating here. You know I can't do carbs. How do I not offend them?"

Gigi started to answer, but her aunt stopped and turned. "Annelise, you eat what you want to. I'll make sure there is salad, too. But, you are a stunning woman, don't starve yourself into a size your body doesn't want to be. Real men like a little padding, don't they, Alessandro?"

"You are more beautiful every year we're together, Elise," Alessandro said, giving his wife a sexy smile and a wink.

Gigi looked at Annelise to gauge her reaction to the open flirtation from the older couple, and they both started laughing. They weren't mocking Alessandro and his wife; it was joyful laughter that came from witnessing something beautiful and fun. *That's what I want. What I need as much as any zing.*

Elise sent Alessandro ahead of them to make sure the parlor was set with finger sandwiches and drinks. When he was out of earshot, she adjusted her loose curls and said, "The day you get engaged, Gigi, I'll give you the talk my mother gave me." Annelise rounded her eyes comically and Elise added, "You, too, Annelise. Every woman should learn from the generation before. The young think they invented love and sex, but you would not be here if that were true, yes?"

Gigi chuckled again. Even though she had held back a hug until she was sure her niece would be comfortable, Elise didn't hold her opinions back.

With a mischievous glint in her eyes, Annelise said, "I'd love some tips."

Elise led the way through the large foyer. "Not until you're engaged, Annelise. We don't waste family secrets on lovers whose names you won't remember later. Use a condom. Be safe. We'll talk when you've found the man you intend to spend the rest of your life with."

Annelise's jaw dropped open, and she whispered again, "I think she's serious." When Elise glanced over her shoulder, Annelise giggled like a guilty child. "And her hearing is exceptional."

Gigi nodded with a smile. "That won't be for a while, Aunt Elise."

Elise stopped at the entry to the parlor. "You never know, Gigi. Love has a way of surprising all of us."

Gigi didn't have time to reflect on Elise's comment. Uncle Victor and his wife, Katrine, were in the parlor and stood and came over as soon as they spotted Gigi. They each hugged her. When Gigi introduced Annelise to them there was just the briefest of awkward moments as if they were sizing each other up.

Annelise threw out her arms and gave each of them a hearty embrace that put smiles on their faces. She mouthed to Gigi, "When in Rome." And Gigi couldn't suppress the huge smile that spread across her face.

Gigi looked around. Although she was happy about it, she was also surprised to see that her uncles and aunts were the only others in the room. During the month she'd been in the States she'd realized inviting one Andrade often meant ten. Inviting ten meant fifty. Anything called a family gathering was well over a hundred. "Is it just us today?"

"Sit. Sit," Alessandro said then addressed her question after everyone was seated. "We told the family to come this afternoon. When you called it sounded as if you wanted to talk. That can be difficult once the house fills up.

Katrine leaned over toward Annelise. "Do you like to cook?"

Annelise made a face and said cautiously, "In theory."

Elise nodded and also stood as if saying she agreed with what Katrine was doing. "You have to meet Richard. My son-in-law is arguably the best chef in North America. In five minutes of watching him you will learn more than you would in a year of cooking classes."

With a straight face, Annelise asked, "Am I allowed to? Are you sure I shouldn't wait until I'm engaged? What if I use what I learn to feed men I won't remember?"

Katrine cocked her head at her in confusion.

Elise cackled and linked arms with Annelise. "You're funny. I like that. And you're still single? Katrine, what about Tino's son? Did he break up with his girlfriend? He's her age."

Katrine and Elise flanked Annelise as they walked out of the room. "I can't see her with Tino. How about Sal's boy? He doesn't speak English, but that has its benefits, too. Love doesn't require translation."

Annelise glanced back at Gigi one final time. She was laughing, but she mouthed, "Help me."

Gigi put up her hands in an apologetic gesture that showed she didn't know how. Once they were alone, Gigi turned back toward her uncles. For the first few minutes she fielded simple questions with ease. They discussed the private plane she'd used to fly over. Although they didn't seem to like that she and Annelise had checked into a hotel, they didn't push her to change her mind and stay with family.

When their conversation hit a lull, Alessandro sat back in his chair and studied Gigi for a long moment. "You look like you have something on your mind, Gigi."

Gigi looked down at her hands momentarily then across at the open expressions on her uncles' faces. "I do." She cleared her throat. "I was hoping you could answer a few questions about my father and his wife."

Victor looked at Alessandro quickly.

Alessandro's face tightened slightly. "Gigi, neither is with us anymore. Let the past go with them."

Gigi gripped the arms of her chair until her knuckles were white. "I would if I could. I don't want to be angry anymore. I want to forget what I know and rewrite my childhood. I don't want to be the daughter of your brother's mistress. Every time I look at my mother I ask myself why she settled for so little. Tell me my father loved her. Explain to me what I have spent my whole life not able to understand." She wiped away quiet tears that had begun to run down her cheeks.

Victor started to say something, but Alessandro put up a hand to silence him. "There are many kinds of love, Gigi. I used to pass judgment on which were moral and which were not, but now I leave that to God to decide. You are old enough to remember what your parents were like when they were together. Were they happy?"

Gigi wiped away another tear as she remembered the smile on her mother's face each time her father returned to them. How their house would be full of laughter while he was there. "Yes, I believe they were. But when I look back at that time, I am so angry. None of it was real. We weren't his real family. How do I stop being angry about that?"

Victor's eyes shone with emotion. "Gigi, people are going to hurt and disappoint you. It's part of life. You can't control that. What you can change is what's in your heart. When we were young, I made a terrible mistake with Patrice, your father's wife. They weren't married, but it was wrong. I have regretted it every day since. She let that one event shape the rest of her life—even taint the last moments with her sons. Who are you punishing with your anger, Gigi? Your father? He's gone. Your mother? Maybe. My guess is the person you're hurting the most is yourself."

Gigi didn't say anything, but inwardly she agreed. Her mother still missed her father, but she was at peace with his death. Gigi, on the other hand, still felt he had abandoned them.

Alessandro looked at Victor with approval, then back at Gigi. "Your mother comes across as a woman who knows her own heart and speaks her mind."

Gigi let out a shaky sigh. "That's true."

Alessandro gave his niece a gentle smile. "Then, perhaps, being like her is not a bad thing, no?"

In a tight voice, Victor said, "If any of us could go back in time and do things differently, we would. But what would the cost be? If we had done everything right, we wouldn't have you."

Gigi smiled through her tears. "My mother said almost

the same thing."

"See," Alessandro said with conviction, "she is very wise."

Gigi nodded. "I'm beginning to see that." It might have been because the talk she'd had with her mother was still fresh in her mind or because her uncles had spoken to her so frankly, but something inside Gigi shifted. Although she didn't agree with anyone being with a married man, her uncle was right. Passing judgment on her parents hadn't hurt them nearly as much as it had her.

It had paralyzed her heart and caused so much bitterness to grow. That wasn't who she used to be. She had been happy when her father had been alive and with them. She did remember so many good times and had never felt like she was second best or unimportant to him. *I had been loved unconditionally, just like these men seem to love me now. Can I let my anger go? Do I have a choice really? Have I lost that chance at love?*

Misunderstanding Gigi's suddenly sad expression, Victor waved a hand dismissively through the air. "Ack, don't worry. It takes most children a long time to realize that their parents may have done one or two things correctly."

"I should go check on Annelise."

Alessandro smiled with amusement. "Tell your friend if she wants a husband, she should learn to cook like my grandmother. With the right sauce recipe a woman can have her pick of men to marry."

Gigi stopped on her way to the door to reprimand him. "Really, Uncle Alessandro? That's all it takes?"

Alessandro smiled widely and shrugged. "Men are easy.

It's women who complicate things."

Gigi wagged a finger at him, but she couldn't deny his claim.

I lost Kane because I was too afraid to admit how I felt about him.

I told myself it was because he didn't look for my mother's possessions, but how ridiculous is that? He spent a month in Edinburgh with me. He respected my decision to wait before having sex again.

He was wonderful to me. We had amazing chemistry. I started missing him the moment he left.

So, of course, I had to end it.

What would he say if I called him now? Asked him to forgive me for being a fool. I don't care if he doesn't want to tame dragons. I'm a strong, independent woman. I can tame my own.

My mother never gave up on anything or anyone she cared about just because it was difficult.

Not my father.

Not my education.

Not even me when I deserved a smack more than her understanding.

She loved us all unconditionally. That takes courage.

I couldn't see that through my anger, but I see it now.

Is it too late to say I'm sorry?

To Mamma.

To Kane.

How do I begin to explain what I'm only now coming to understand?

Love isn't something I've done well, but I can do it better.

I will do it better.

✧ ✧ ✧

KANE HUNG UP with Max and threw the paper he'd been taking notes on down onto the kitchen table of his apartment. Gigi's spur-of-the-moment arrival in New York had changed the timeline of their plan.

He called his jeweler and put a rush on the ring. Forget about the week or two he'd said was fine. He needed it by the weekend. It could have been Kane's tone or the amount of money he was paying for the ring, but the jeweler didn't balk at the request.

Several phone calls later, Kane was satisfied that everything would still go smoothly. He shrugged off his suit jacket, stepped out of his shoes, and had started to unbutton his shirt when his cell phone rang.

Gigi.

He cleared his throat and tried to sound calmer than he felt when he answered. "Hello, Gigi."

"Kane."

Kane closed his eyes at the simple pleasure of hearing her say his name. "I heard you're in New York."

She didn't answer for a moment, then said softly, "I'm downstairs. May I come up?"

Yes. Yes. Hell yes.

He buzzed her in. She hung up after he gave her the number to his apartment. He stood there, his cock swelling with excitement, his chest tight with anticipation, and told himself to not to rush her. This was not the plan, but it would still work. She probably wanted to explain what he'd overheard in Edinburgh.

Possibly apologize for hurting him.

She wouldn't be ready for what his dick was hoping for.

He was at the door a heartbeat after her soft knock. She was holding a plastic food container in her hands. The room sizzled as their eyes met.

She smiled shyly. "I went to see my uncles today. I brought you a container of leftovers." Like Kane, Gigi looked as if she was having difficulty concentrating on anything beyond the attraction between them. Her voice became husky. "Just some pasta and sauce."

He stepped closer to take it from her. When his hands closed over hers, he groaned audibly. His need for her was scattering the last of his sanity. They stood in the doorway, both holding the plastic container between them.

"I've missed you, Gigi," he admitted.

She stepped back, releasing the container to him, and he cursed himself for pushing her before she had time to say why she'd come.

Gigi closed the door behind her then gave him a sexy little smile that took his breath away. She bit her bottom lip deliciously, and he practically came at the memory of how those lips had felt around his cock. "I'm sorry about what I said."

Kane opened his mouth to say . . . really he had no idea what he would say, but he hoped it would be what she wanted to hear. Before he could utter a sound she placed a finger across his lips to silence him.

He swallowed hard.

She started to unbutton her blouse as she spoke. "I

missed you, too." She slid her shirt off and tossed it on the floor beside her, then reached back to release her bra and threw that aside also. "There is so much I want to say, but can it wait? Right now I just want to be with you."

The food container hit the floor, and Kane pulled Gigi into his arms for a kiss he'd remember the rest of his life. All the waiting had built a need within him unlike any he'd felt before. They kissed as lovers do after a painfully long separation. He couldn't get enough of her. His mouth ravaged hers. His hands tore off the rest of her clothing.

She was stripping him just as enthusiastically.

Kane picked her up and carried her to his bedroom, feeling like a conquering warrior about to claim his bounty. He threw her onto the bed, loving the wild hunger in her eyes, the way she didn't try to hide any part of her from him.

He was kneeling above her, running his hands over her with a roughness that matched his desire for her, and she moaned in encouragement. Nothing that had occurred before, or what would happen later, mattered. Gigi spread her legs wide for him, and the glisten of her arousal drove him to savor a taste.

She buried her hands in his hair, writhing against his mouth. He claimed her sex mercilessly with his tongue and his teeth, as his hands closed over her hips and held her to him. She was sweeter than he remembered, more powerfully addictive than before. Had she denied him then, he doubted he could have survived the pain.

When she came in his mouth it was the sweetest nectar. *How have I survived without her taste?* He massaged her sensitive clit with his thumb, and drove his tongue deeper and deeper inside her until she was crying out his name again and digging her nails into his shoulders.

When she was quickly approaching another orgasm, he raised himself above her and plunged his cock into her. She cried out for him to take her harder, and he did. He held nothing back, pounding into her with a force he normally would have reined back.

She wrapped herself around him, meeting his thrusts with a frenzy that matched his own. He leaned down and kissed her, loving how she opened herself to him completely. He made love to her mouth with the same intensity.

When an orgasm shook through him, he tried to hold it off, but he couldn't. With one last powerful thrust, he came, loving how she tightened around his cock and shuddered with her own release.

He stayed above her, inside her, looking down into the most beautiful wild eyes he'd ever seen. As his breathing slowly returned to normal, he gave her a lusty smile and said, "You're forgiven."

Chapter Twenty-One

BLISS was the only word Gigi could think of to describe how she felt in Kane's arms. When she'd left Annelise at their hotel suite, she'd told her she wouldn't be late. She'd planned to apologize to Kane and then talk to him.

She'd planned to keep her clothing on.

Gigi closed her eyes and sighed with pleasure when Kane cuddled her closer to his side and kissed her bare shoulder. Being with him had felt right the first time, but this had been mind-blowingly right. An orgasmic epiphany.

"Shit," Kane said with a harshness that made Gigi's eyes fly open. "I didn't use a condom."

Gigi tensed, but didn't know what the proper response to that revelation was? She'd love to announce she was on birth control, but she wasn't. Outside of Kane, she hadn't needed to be in a very long time. "I'm sure it will be fine."

Kane didn't loosen his hold on her, but his expression had changed. He wasn't happy. "I don't make mistakes like this. And you shouldn't either. There are way too many risks involved."

Gigi sat up and pushed her hair back from her face.

"First of all, I don't usually worry about birth control because I haven't slept with anyone since college. Second of all, I don't like your tone—"

A grin spread across Kane's face, and he spoke over her. "When did you graduate? Three years ago?"

He looked so happy about it; Gigi was torn between irritation and amusement. "A little more than that."

"So you haven't been with anyone since you met me."

Gigi rolled her eyes and swatted Kane's chest. "A coincidence."

He rolled her on top of him. "Maybe, but one I like."

Gigi propped herself up with a hand on either side of his head. "What about you?"

With feigned innocence, Kane kissed her shoulder and asked, "Have I mentioned how beautiful you are?"

"You think I'm that easy to distract?" Gigi went to move off him, but he held her where she was and took one of her nipples gently between his teeth. He tugged on it lightly while running his tongue back and forth across its tip. Whatever annoyance she'd felt dissolved as a wave of desire rocked through her. She moved her hips back and forth over his hardening shaft, loving how he felt against the lips of her wet sex.

They kissed and rolled. Teased and caressed. Neither was capable of a coherent sentence while they explored each other's body. The first time had been rushed. This time was a slow, worshipping exploration.

When being intimately connected was all either of them could think about, Kane knocked over a lamp trying to locate his condoms. He slid one on just before he entered her. Together they found a rhythm that brought them both to heaven and back.

Later, with their bare legs entwined and Gigi's head resting on Kane's shoulder, Gigi lacked the words to describe how sated she felt.

Kane caressed her back lazily with one hand. "Gigi. I want to wake up to you every morning and fall sleep each night with you in my arms. I've never wanted that with any other woman. That's what matters."

Gigi kissed his chest. "I know. I won't make the same mistake again."

Kane raised his head. "What mistake was that?"

Gigi shook her head. "It doesn't matter."

Kane put one hand beneath Gigi's chin and raised her face so she was forced to meet his eyes. "It does to me. What won't you do again?"

Gigi chewed her bottom lip as she chose her words. She did want him to understand what she'd learned since she'd last seen him. "I was holding people to unrealistic expectations. I see that now. I could give you a list of excuses why I was like that, but they don't matter anymore. I appreciate you for the man you are, Kane. You don't have to fulfill any ridiculous quest to prove to me that you care about me."

"Quest . . . are you referring to your mother's things?"

Gigi looked away, embarrassed she was so transparent. "I told you it was ridiculous."

Kane sat up and frowned down at her. "I love you, Gigi."

"I love you, too." She scooted up to kiss him, but he

stopped her midway. "What's wrong, Kane?"

"This is all wrong. I don't want you to lower your expectations of me."

Confused, Gigi gathered the sheet up around herself. "Kane?"

Kane slid off the bed and stepped into his pants. "I need to think about this, and I can't do that with you next to me."

Gigi wrapped the sheet around herself and stood. Fight them as she tried, tears began to spill over. "Kane. You said you loved me. I said it back. Why are you upset?"

Kane picked up Gigi's clothes and handed them to her. "This doesn't feel right."

Numb with the pain spreading through her, Gigi put on her clothes. "Really? Well, I'm glad we've realized this before I made a complete ass of myself and let you trample all over my heart. You're a real piece of work, you know that, Kane? Is this your idea of some sick game? I hurt you in Edinburgh, so you do this to me?"

Gigi pushed past Kane and made it all the way to the door of his apartment before he caught up to her. He made a grab for her arm, but she eluded him. "Gigi, don't go like this. You don't understand."

"I understand more than you think I do," Gigi said angrily. She looked at the container of pasta and sauce and was angry for believing for one moment that Alessandro's method would work with Kane. Angry with herself. Angry with Kane. Gigi opened the container and threw the contents first and then the container at him. "Here, have your damn sauce."

He looked more shocked than angry, but Gigi didn't wait for that to change. She stormed out of his apartment and down to the lobby to call for a car. Her emotions were a tornado of confusion and hurt.

It wasn't until she was back at her hotel and retelling the story to Annelise that she started to cry. "He said my love didn't feel right. What does that even mean?"

Annelise poured a glass of wine for each of them. "It means he deserved to wear that pasta."

✧ ✧ ✧

KANE PACED HIS apartment as he rehashed what had happened with Gigi. He knew she misunderstood what he'd said. He groaned as he remembered how he'd voiced his thoughts. What he meant to say was *he wanted to be given a chance* to prove his love to her. That she deserved a man who would do anything for her. He didn't want her to see him as a man she could love even if he disappointed her. He wanted to be her champion. He should have told her he'd just recently completed gathering every item her mother had sold off, and the most expensive painting was presently hanging in the house Max had bought for her several years ago. A house that was proof of how much her brothers loved her. It was tangible evidence that she was one of them.

Just as the painting he'd hung in that house was proof Kane was the man Gigi had hoped he would be.

He'd wanted to tell her all of that, but he also hadn't wanted to rob her of the experience. Hearing about what they had planned for her wouldn't have the same effect as going to that house and seeing it for herself.

Declarations of love and promises of forever were supposed to come after she understood how precious she was to him. Not before.

That's what had felt wrong.

He sent her a text, but she didn't answer it. He called her, but she didn't pick up.

I don't think I got my point across well.

Chapter Twenty-Two

THE NEXT MORNING Gigi was packing to leave for the airport when her cell phone rang. It was one of her brothers. She sat on the edge of her bed and answered grumpily, "Hi, Luke."

"Heard you were in New York. Cassie and I are, too. Would you like to meet for lunch?"

"Annelise and I are flying out in a couple hours."

"Delay your flight. We want to see you."

Gigi's throat tightened with emotion. She'd spent a sleepless night trying not to think about Kane and what he'd said. She wouldn't let it come between her and her brothers, but she did need some time to put it behind her before she could face them. "I can't." She regretted how much she'd revealed with her voice.

"What happened, Gigi? Are you okay?"

"I'm fine. I need to get out of New York."

"That works with my next suggestion. We're having a family gathering on Slater Island on Saturday, and we'd like you to be there. Cassie and I could fly out there with you today."

Slater Island? That was the last place she wanted to be. She'd never be able to go there without thinking of the first time she met Kane. "Sorry, Luke. Another time."

Across the room Annelise halted packing her case and raised her eyes. She walked over, took the phone away from Gigi, and said, "Hi, Luke. It's Annelise. What is Gigi turning down?"

Gigi tried to grab her phone, but Annelise walked away with it. She spoke to Luke for about ten minutes before walking back near Gigi. "That all sounds perfect. We'll fly in Saturday morning. Gigi owes me a tour of New York, and I'm not leaving without one." She laughed at something Luke said. "Great. Looking forward to seeing you again."

Gigi was fuming by the time Annelise hung up with Luke. "What was that about? I said I didn't want to go."

Annelise folded her arms across her chest. "I didn't get dragged halfway around the world to attend whatever pity party you're planning for yourself. You always tell me you value my honesty, but you might not like it this time. Life didn't cheat you, Gigi. You have a wonderful mother. You're healthy. You're beautiful. And now you're rich without having done anything for that fortune. It's really hard to listen to you whine." Annelise scrolled through Gigi's phone. "You have brothers who want to be with you, but you turn away from them. Kane called you . . . five times? But instead of taking his calls you'd rather stay upset with him." When Gigi opened her mouth to bring up what Kane had said the night before, Annelise waved it off. "I don't care what he said last night. I've seen him with you. He's crazy about you. You are your own worst enemy, Gigi. If you don't figure out how to get out of your own way, you're going lose everything. And it won't be anyone's fault but yours." She tossed Gigi's phone back to her. "Call Kane."

Gigi looked down at her phone. "I'm scared, Annelise. I don't want to be my own worst enemy."

Annelise walked over and put an arm around Gigi's shoulder. "You think you're alone in that feeling? I'm twenty-five years old, and I've never had a relationship last longer than a month. I weigh myself five times a day because I'm terrified I'll go back to the size I was in high school. I thought I had a career until my business partner decided her personal life trumped work, and now I'm along for a ride that will end, but I don't know how, and *I don't know when*. So, pull your shit together, Gigi. Because I need you every bit as much as you need me, and I'm beginning to freak out."

Looking at the last month through Annelise's eyes was a wakeup call for Gigi. "How do you put up with me?"

Annelise gave her a small smile. "You're my best friend, and you always will be. You've weathered through my tough times. I'm not leaving you during yours. I wish I had the answers for you in this situation. I don't. I just hate to see you walk away from your chance to have the life you always said you wanted because you're scared. Life is scary. So what are we going to do, curl up in a corner and hide from it? Give your brothers a chance to be there for you and let Kane apologize if that's what he's trying to do. Have a little faith in them, and they just might surprise you."

After giving Annelise a long, grateful hug, Gigi sat down on the edge of her bed and called Kane. He picked up on the first ring.

✧   ✧   ✧

KANE HAD BEEN up all night cursing himself for not explaining his feelings better to Gigi. The more he thought about what he'd said and how he'd said it, the more he didn't blame her for throwing food at him. Somewhere around two o'clock in the morning, Kane had called Gio.

"Am I your one phone call because you were caught doing something illegal?" Gio had asked gruffly.

"No," Kane had answered slowly.

"Are you in the hospital? Is anyone we know awaiting an emergency procedure?"

"Nothing like that. I need to tell you something. I'm going to ask Gigi to marry me on Slater Island this weekend."

"Who is it?" Julia had asked in the background.

"It's Kane," Gio said grumpily, sounding every bit like a man who had been woken from sleep and wasn't happy about it. "He's going to ask Gigi to marry him. Are you looking for my blessing?"

"Yes and no, I will marry her either way. But it would mean a lot to me to know that you approve. Loving Gigi has opened my eyes. My father always said family meant more to him than anything else could. I believed him, but I didn't get it. I understand now. Nothing matters more to me than Gigi's happiness. You're a part of that. I'm a part of it. It's all connected and I want to make sure I move forward with Gigi in a way that brings all of us closer."

Gio sighed. "My sister had better say yes, because she will never find a better man. I'm going back to sleep, Kane. We're good." Before he hung up, he added, "Julia suggested you fly Leora in for the weekend. She said if you're going to propose, her mother should be there, too. I'd do it. Julia's good with these kind of things."

◆ ◆ ◆

AFTER HANGING UP with Gio, Kane had called Leora and explained his plans for the weekend. She was enthusiastic, but not surprised. She said she'd known from the first time she'd seen them together they were perfect for each other. Her positive response, added to Gio's acceptance, confirmed what Kane already knew—he and Gigi were meant to be.

At four a.m. Kane acknowledged to himself that the plan he'd hatched with Nick and his brothers had a higher likelihood of success before Gigi stopped accepting his phone calls. He thought about the women he'd been with before her. Sex and relationships had come easily to him. Rather than looking for ways to win them over, he'd fought to keep things casual.

He'd never worked this hard to be with a woman.

He'd never cared enough to want to.

Gigi was different. She wasn't just a woman he wanted to be with, she was the only woman he wanted. Part of loving Gigi was embracing her uniqueness and wanting all of her, even the parts he was still trying to understand. He had been raised in a close family. Neither he nor Rena had ever known a day of rejection or fear. They'd never struggled financially, had never felt abandoned.

When he imagined what it must have been like for Gigi to be raised outside of her family, hidden and ashamed, his heart broke for her. Was it any wonder she didn't like surprises? She'd had enough unpleasant ones.

She didn't trust people easily, but she'd been given reasons not to. Once he started looking at their exchanges through her eyes, he knew exactly how he would win her back.

He was dressed and heading out the door to go to her when his phone rang. He almost dropped it when he realized who it was and rushed to answer it. "Gigi," Kane said with forced calmness.

"Is this a bad time?" Gigi asked tentatively.

"Never. I was coming to you."

She was quiet for a moment. "You were?"

The hope in her voice sent a rush of warmth through Kane. "I may have done many things, but I have never lied to you, and I never will."

"I want to explain what I did last night."

"You mean dousing me with sauce?"

She made a pained sound. "I'm sorry about that. No matter how upset I get, I don't throw things. I don't know what came over me."

"You were angry."

"Yes."

"And scared."

Gigi was quiet for another long pause, then she admitted

softly, "Yes. I didn't know what to do when you said my love didn't feel right."

"I didn't—" Kane stopped himself. This wasn't about being right or wrong. He loved her and was willing to meet her more than halfway if she needed him to. "I didn't express myself well last night. I know what I want, Gigi. I want you. I love you. Pack an overnight bag. I want to show you something, and I don't think you'll want to leave once you see it."

"I can't go anywhere. I have Annelise with me," Gigi said slowly.

"Bring her," Kane said firmly. "Tell her to pack an overnight bag, also. I know you don't like surprises, Gigi, but give me a chance to show you what I failed miserably at explaining last night. I'll be by to pick you up in an hour."

"I didn't agree to go."

Kane wasn't about to let that stop him. "One more thing. What's your favorite flower?"

"I don't know that I have one."

Kane didn't hesitate. "You remind me of white roses: honest, loyal, strong."

Gigi laughed softly in self-derision. "That's the me I want to be."

A year ago Kane wouldn't have understood what she meant. He would have seen her uncertainty as weakness. He used to think he had all the answers, but Gigi had opened his eyes to how much he didn't know. Yes, she had emotional scars and fears left over from her childhood, but they only made her more beautiful to him. "I'm on my way now."

Kane hung up. He wasn't giving himself a chance to say anything that would stop her from flying off to Slater Island with him. She might think she didn't need him to prove anything to her, but she was wrong. That's what had felt wrong.

He wouldn't settle for being less than her hero.

Chapter Twenty-Three

GIGI DIDN'T KNOW what to expect when Rocco, her security guard, called to announce Kane's arrival. Her stomach was doing somersaults. Part of her wanted so badly to believe this was the beginning of a real future with Kane. Part of her froze at the idea of opening her heart to him again.

Annelise was beside her with her overnight bag. "Are you going to open the door when he knocks or barricade it?"

Gigi looked across at her friend. "Am I that transparent?"

Annelise gave a knowing look. "You can do this. I've seen you handle feisty customers with ease. Do you remember during our freshman year at Kensington Academy when they announced they were no longer allowing students to choose their own roommates? You fought all the way up to the headmaster and won. You, Gigi. Most of us called our parents and had them contact the headmaster, but you took on that battle yourself."

Gigi grimaced. "My mother had enough on her plate. She was already working a second job to pay for my schooling."

"That's my point. You're stronger than you think. You're also the kindest and most loyal person I know. You deserve this. Yes, you had a tough childhood, but it made you who you are. You don't have to wish you were a white rose, you are one."

Annelise's pep talk was interrupted by a knock on the hotel room door. Gigi shot her friend a grateful smile and said to herself, "I am a white rose." Annelise gave her a thumbs up. Gigi squared her shoulders and walked over to open the door.

Dressed in jeans and a black T-shirt that accentuated his muscular chest, Kane stood there proudly holding the largest bouquet of white roses she'd ever seen. It wasn't just the flowers, though, that moved her the most. It was the expression in his eyes. Every bit of emotion she'd yearned to see in them was openly displayed.

He handed the flowers to Annelise, took Gigi's face between his hands and gave her a kiss so tender tears filled Gigi's eyes. She threw her arms around his neck and kissed him back with all the questions, the yearning, and the love churning inside her.

"I'll put these in water," Annelise said dryly from behind them.

When the kiss ended they stood there in each other's arms, breathing heavily and unable to look away. One of his strong hands was buried beneath her hair. The other still cupped her face, and he wiped away one of her tears with his thumb. "Don't run away again, Gigi. This time stay, and let me show you why we belong together."

"Call me when you get back," Annelise said from beside them.

"No," Kane said firmly without looking away from Gigi. "Come with us. We're staying overnight, and you should be there tomorrow."

"Okay," Annelise said slowly. "Listen, I love you, Gigi. I'd do anything for you. And I like you, Kane. But this has that awkward, third wheel, I don't want to be trapped while you two maul each other, feel about it. I'm perfectly fine waiting here until you come back."

Kane stepped back, took one of Gigi's hands in his, raised it to his mouth, and kissed it lightly. Then he turned to Annelise and smiled. "I can control myself." He gave Gigi's hand a gentle squeeze and met her eyes. "Especially since I'm hoping for a lifetime of mauling."

Gigi's breath caught in her throat. *Did he just say what I thought he said?* Her eyes flew to her friend for confirmation. The approving expression on Annelise's face confirmed that she had. *Holy Moly. He's going to propose. And if he wants Annelise there, it means he has something planned for how he'll do it.* In a slightly strangled voice, Gigi said, "Annelise, please come with us."

Annelise picked up her overnight bag and shook her head in amusement. "I'll go, but you two need to keep your hands off each other, or I swear I'll throw a glass of water on you both."

Kane barked out a laugh.

Gigi squeezed his hand between both of hers. "She'd do it, you know."

Kane pulled Gigi to his side for an affectionate hug. "I bet she would. I like you, too, Annelise. Now let's go. I have a helicopter waiting for us on the roof." While still holding Gigi's hand, Kane picked up her luggage.

Even though the destination had zero chance of changing her mind, Gigi asked, "Where are we going?"

They stepped out of the hotel room and took an elevator up to the roof. Kane waited until they were bent over and rushing beneath the spinning blades of the executive helicopter before he answered. "Slater Island."

Gigi was already seated beside Kane inside the lavish silver and ivory interior by the time his answer sunk in. Did he have to choose where she'd made a fool of herself? If he was going to propose she could think of a thousand places she'd rather go. She didn't want to think about how she'd felt at her brothers' weddings, toward him or toward them. Couldn't they put all that behind them? "I'd rather not go there."

From a seat across from her, Annelise looked on with sympathy. Moments like that made Gigi glad she told her friend everything. She didn't have to explain herself to Annelise. Gigi turned to Kane and hoped she could make him understand as well. "Especially if you're about to do what I think you might be about to do, let's not do it on that island."

Kane studied her expression closely. "You don't like Slater Island? It's where we met."

Gigi looked away in embarrassment. "Have you forgotten how that went?"

Kane shook his head and laced his fingers with hers. "All I remember about that night is meeting an incredibly sexy Italian woman who would haunt my dreams for the next three years."

Gigi's eyes flew back to his. She blushed, but with a mix of hope and excitement. She challenged him, hoping to hear a version that would make it all right. "You turned me down. And you laughed at me when you did it."

He kissed the knuckles of one of her hands then said, "I laughed at myself for not seeing how young you were. Trust me, there was nothing funny about walking away from you that night. I wanted you then just as badly as I do now."

Annelise cleared her throat. "We are quickly approaching the intersection of 'this is awkward to listen to, and I wish I hadn't come.'"

Gigi and Kane exchanged a guilty smile and most of Gigi's anxiety slipped away. They turned back to look at Annelise and said in unison, "Sorry." Then glanced at each other and burst out laughing.

Annelise rolled her eyes. "I'll give you two points for being adorable together, but don't forget I'm here and armed with a water bottle."

✧ ✧ ✧

KANE WATCHED GIGI and Annelise laugh together over her comment, and he knew bringing her had been the right choice. Their friendship was a source of strength for Gigi, and he wanted that to be part of his future with her. His parents had always maintained that love wasn't competitive or limiting. Not when it was right.

It was amazing how advice he'd brushed off before suddenly fit. Annelise had offered to stay behind. He could have agreed with her, and the ride over to the island might have involved a whole lot less clothing. It might have been a night to remember, but it wouldn't have been what Gigi needed.

For the first time in his life, the needs of a woman overshadowed his own. That didn't mean he didn't want her so much he ached for her, but it did mean her happiness came first. In the past, he'd used the word love with a couple of women. He'd walked away from them. They'd walked away from him. He'd always moved on easily, and now he understood why.

He loved Gigi. He shook his head. The word love couldn't fully express how he felt about her. Which was why he was taking her to Slater Island. He needed to show her.

Out of respect for Annelise, Kane brought up more mundane topics for discussion. They spent the next couple hours talking about the places Gigi and Annelise had visited and where they might enjoy going.

When they finally approached Slater Island, the pilot did as Kane had instructed and circled the bluffs where the Andrade homes were. Kane leaned over Gigi. "Do you see those mansions?"

She tensed against him. "I see them," Gigi said and turned away from the view of them. Her eyes were wild with a panic he was beginning to understand. "You're not showing me anything I haven't already seen."

"The last time you were here, you felt like you didn't belong, but you did," he said softly.

"Can we go somewhere else, Kane? Please."

Kane took her chin in his hand and gently turned it back to the window. "When you look down there you see four Andrade homes, but I see five. That last house, the one just before the curve of the bluffs, that's yours, Gigi. Max bought it for you. It's been waiting for you all this time. If you need proof your brothers love you, it's right there. When they planned a place for their family to gather, they planned for you to be there with them."

Gigi looked at the houses, back at Kane, back at the houses, then at Annelise before focusing once more on the mansion Kane had pointed out to her. "When did he buy it for me?"

"Back when he first learned you existed. They've debated telling you about it often, but they were waiting for the right time to surprise you with it. Your family is having a large Andrade gathering here tomorrow. They're planning to make the announcement to you then."

"That's why they invited me." Her voice was shaky with emotion.

"Yes, and because they know I intend to propose to you tomorrow."

Her eyes rounded with surprise. For a moment she was stunned into silence, then she asked, "Tomorrow? Not today?"

Kane flashed her a gentle smile. "Not today."

Gigi brought a trembling hand up to her lips. "Then why are we here today?"

"Because there is something in your house down there I want you to see before I ask you to marry me."

Gigi looked across at Annelise who shrugged as if saying she had no clue what he was referring to. When Gigi met Kane's eyes again, she was smiling even as her eyes shone with tears. "You don't need to prove anything to me. I love you, and I'm so sorry I doubted you."

He put a finger up to her lips. "I know, Gigi, but let me do this. It took me a while, but I understand now. With me, Gigi, you'll never have to wonder, you'll never have to doubt, you'll never have to wish again. You'll know I love you. I'll spend the rest of my life happily showing you."

Gigi took his hand in hers, held it to the side of her face and gave him a teary smile.

From the other side of the helicopter, Annelise sniffed loudly. "I brought a water bottle, but I didn't bring tissues. You guys are killing me here."

Chapter Twenty-Four

Some moments in life are experienced and quickly forgotten. Others are etched on a person's soul, and they are forever changed because of them. Regardless of what Kane would show her on the island, he had broken past her defenses and left her both vulnerable and indescribably stronger.

Love.

She'd thought she understood it. She'd been sure she'd felt it—even recently for Kane. But she realized then what she'd called love had been merely the beginning of something much, much more beautiful.

Every sappy movie she'd ever watched suddenly made sense. What she felt for Kane was so intense; she doubted it could be contained in one lifetime. Looking deeply into his eyes she suddenly felt truly free for the first time since her father's death.

Free from the anger she'd tried and failed so many times to put behind her.

Free from insecurities she'd denied, but had succumbed to again and again in moments of weakness.

Kane saw her, really saw her, and accepted what she considered her greatest flaws. She didn't know how she'd ever thank him for that, but she knew she'd spend the rest of her life trying to.

The helicopter landed on the lawn of the home Kane had said was hers. Kane helped Gigi and Annelise out then walked with both of them to the steps of the mansion.

Annelise looked around and said, "I'll wait out here."

Kane encouraged her to join them but Annelise waved a hand toward the house and laughed. "I have a feeling that whatever you're about to show her is going to end with a kiss, that I'm completely okay with missing. I will say, though, that if you two don't get married, I am giving up on love."

Gigi closed the distance between her and her best friend and gave her a bone-crushing, grateful hug. "Don't wait out here. Come inside with us."

Annelise hugged her back tightly and whispered, "I have my cell phone. I'm sure this island has a cab service. I'm actually excited to do a little sightseeing."

Gigi pulled back and studied Annelise's expression. "You're sure?"

Annelise looked over at Kane and said, "If our roles were reversed, I'd ditch you in a heartbeat. I'm fine. I don't want to miss a moment of his proposal tomorrow, but you and Kane need a little alone time. I'm fine. Now go. Get outta here."

Gigi stopped before walking away. "Ask for Waffle."

"For what?"

"Not what. Who. When you call for a cab, ask for the driver named Waffle."

Annelise looked at Gigi as if waiting for the punch line. "Seriously?"

Gigi smiled. Just as Kane had brought a calm to her by loving her despite her flaws, Gigi could imagine Waffle loving a woman the same way. She didn't know if Annelise could be that woman, but what she'd learned over the past few months was that you can't know unless you take a chance. Gigi couldn't imagine how she would feel had she not allowed Kane to take her home to meet her brothers.

It was impossible to know which leaps of faith would pay off and which would end in disappointment, but Gigi decided she would never again let that hold her back. Life was a whole hell of a lot better when not hiding from it. "And if he offers you a slice of pie, taste it."

"You know I don't eat—"

Gigi cut her off and gave her one more quick hug. "Do it this time. Trust me."

After Annelise shrugged and searched her phone for the number, Gigi turned back to Kane. He was waiting patiently for her with a grin on his face.

"Ready?" he asked.

She placed her hand in his and walked up the steps of the large stone mansion with him. It wasn't as large as Gio and Julia's home, but it was impressive by anyone's standards. He typed in a code on the security system and opened the door.

Instead of following him inside, Gigi tugged on his hand until he turned to face her. "You don't have to wait until tomorrow to hear my answer. I'll marry you, Kane."

His smile widened, and he kissed the tip of her nose. "That is not how this works. I went to a great deal of trouble to make sure everything is perfect. You will follow me inside, be suitably shocked, hopefully decadently grateful, and then we'll come back here tomorrow and do this all over again with your family here. Except the X-rated part. We'll save that for after they leave."

Gigi loved the laughter in his eyes and the way he demanded she go exactly where they both knew she wanted to. "You're rather bossy today."

"Is that a complaint?" he growled softly and pulled her into his arms, nuzzling her neck.

"Oh, no," Gigi said and went onto her tiptoes to deliver the kiss she'd been yearning to give but had held back from out of respect for Annelise. "But it makes me want to skip right to the good part."

He was instantly hard, and she wasn't joking.

He shuddered against her. "I'm trying to do this the right way."

"Who is to say this isn't it?" His lack of control around her was a powerful aphrodisiac. Gigi ran her hands up and down his chest, loving how she could feel his heart thudding wildly. Their clothing was an almost painful barrier between them. Gigi wanted to feel his hands on her bare skin. Her hands on his. She pulled his shirt out of his trousers and slid her hands up his taut stomach.

From the driveway, Annelise called out, "I'm taking my bag with me. I'll spend the night in town. You two lovebirds don't need to worry about me."

Gigi would have answered her, but Kane swept her up in his arms, stepped through the door, and kicked it shut behind him. The foyer was enormous, but that was all that registered. All that existed for Gigi was Kane. His kiss. His strong touch. They stripped each other without breaking the kiss.

Every caress was better than the last. Each dance of their tongues was sheer heaven. Theirs was a heated, loving mating that rose in tempo like a rhapsody until they were completely lost in the touch and taste of each other. He took her against the wall, thrusting into her as she wrapped herself around him. She cried out as wave after wave of pleasure rocked through her, and he came with one final deep lunge. As they slowly came back to earth, they stayed there, no separation of him or her, just a gloriously sated . . . them.

He finally lowered her back onto her feet, kissing her deeply as he did. "You're dangerous, Gigi."

Gigi smiled, laid her head against his chest, and wrapped her arms around him. Their lovemaking was incredible, but this, just the feeling of him all around her, was another pleasure she knew she'd never get enough of. "And you're amazing. At least we made it inside the door."

She felt rather than heard his chuckle. "Barely."

"We should probably put our clothes back on. Knowing your family, someone is bound to come by to start setting up for tomorrow."

"That would be as bad as what Julia almost caught me doing in the closet on the night of my welcome home party."

Kane raised his head and his eyes burned with an emotion that took Gigi by surprise. He was jealous. "Who were you in a closet with that night?"

Gigi rubbed her naked body against his in an all-over caress. Even though she loved how possessive he was, she didn't want him to imagine what had never and would never happen. "Only myself. I ran into the closet because I needed a moment alone to think, but after what we had shared on the terrace, I was so frustrated I considered taking matters into my own hands, so to speak." She tipped her head back and grinned. "I'm glad I didn't. Julia came in to check on me. It would have made for a very awkward sister-in-law moment."

A slow sexy smile spread across Kane's face. "So you have a closet fetish?"

Gigi laughed, feeling lighthearted and sexy. "No, but if it's the only way to be alone, it works. Here we'd have the whole house."

Kane bent and pulled his cell phone out of his pants pocket. His rippling muscular back and perfectly toned ass were a joy to watch in motion. "I told Rocco to follow us. I'll tell him to stand guard."

Gigi blushed. "He'll know what we're doing."

Kane briefly gave instructions to Gigi's bodyguard then threw his phone onto the pile of his clothing near the door. "How we feel about each other isn't exactly a secret."

Gigi thought of how they'd almost not made it inside the house, and her blush deepened. "You're right, I guess."

Kane pulled her gently into his arms, encircling her waist

and bringing her full against the evidence of his arousal. "I want you again, Gigi. Right now. But I can wait. What do you want to do?"

There it was, the acceptance that gave Gigi the confidence to drop her inhibitions and be herself. She threw her arms back around him and between kisses said, "Let's christen every room in this damn house."

Kane's eyebrows rose. "A house this big could have quite a few."

Gigi fluttered her eyelashes at him and gave his cheek a playfully sympathetic pat. "Oh, and at your age, that's a problem?"

"At my age?" Kane's smile widened at her challenge. "I'll show you what someone my age is capable of." He picked her up and carried her to the first room off the foyer.

✧ ✧ ✧

Two hours later, Kane lay beside Gigi in one of the few beds in the mostly unfurnished home. She was cuddled against him beneath a bed sheet. "We didn't get past the third room."

Completely disheveled and glowing from their lovemaking, Gigi kissed his shoulder and murmured, "One more orgasm and I'm going to drown in a pool of my own drool."

He closed his eyes, enjoying how at peace he felt with the universe. "But what a way to go."

The sound of a helicopter flying over the house broke their comfortable silence. Gigi didn't raise her head. "Do you think that's my family arriving?"

Kane groan without opening his eyes. "Probably."

"Poor Rocco."

Kane hugged Gigi even more closely against his side. "We can shower and dress quickly if you want."

Gigi shook her head. "All I want to do is to stay like this for as long as we can. Then I'd like to go downstairs and see what you brought me here to show me."

What I brought her . . .

"Shit. Gigi. I can't believe I completely forgot about that." He'd never felt like more of an ass. "What happens to my brain when I'm around you?"

Gigi traced his lips with a gentle finger. "I don't know, Kane; I've been the same since the first time I met you."

Kane took her hand in his and brought her wrist to his mouth for a kiss. "I do have something very important to show you." He yawned.

Gigi closed her eyes and her breathing deepened as she fell asleep against him. He held her for a long time, savoring the feeling of her beside him. Voices outside the house kept him from joining her in slumber. At first it was just a couple, then more until it sounded as if a crowd were gathering outside on the lawn.

Kane slipped downstairs to retrieve his clothing. He sent a text to Rocco and his pilot to have their bags brought inside. Once everything was set, he woke Gigi with a warm kiss and dragged her out of bed and into the shower with him.

A short time later, presentably dressed, they walked hand in hand down to the foyer. Gigi wore minimal makeup, but her cheeks still glowed from their lovemaking, and she'd never looked more beautiful.

He led her to the doorway of a sparsely furnished sitting room and covered her eyes with one of his hands while guiding her forward with his other. "In Edinburgh you asked me for my help with something."

Gigi pulled at his hand and protested. "Kane, it doesn't matter."

He kept his hand over her eyes and continued to firmly guide her until she was standing before a large painting on the wall. "Yes, it does." He lowered his hand.

Gigi gasped. "You convinced the collector to sell it? He told me he wouldn't even consider it. Oh my God, Kane, my mother will be so happy. You don't know what this means to me." She turned back to him with eyes that were bright with tears.

He took both of her hands in his. "Don't you dare cry because then I won't tell you that every single item on the list you gave me is sitting in a warehouse near Venice. I thought this painting would be the perfect way for you to tell your mother that her palazzo will be complete again."

Tears ran freely down Gigi's cheeks. She threw her arms around him and hugged him tightly. "I didn't think I could love you more, but I was wrong. I don't know how to begin to thank you."

Kane put a finger beneath her chin and raised her face to meet his. "Tomorrow when I ask you to marry me, say yes."

"Are you sure you don't want to ask me now?"

A younger Kane would have, but loving Gigi had also

taught him patience. "Leora will be here tomorrow. When I first met your mother she asked me for two things. Both felt impossible, but now I see they aren't. They never were."

Gigi cocked her head in confusion. "Did my mother ask you to marry me?"

Kane shook his head. "No. She asked me to bring Gigi to her brothers and Gigia home to her. I didn't understand her request or you much at the time, but now I do. When I asked your brothers if they would be okay with Leora being here, they said they welcomed her into their family years ago because she is part of you. I can't begin to try to unravel what happened between Patrice and her sons, or your mother and your father, but I know it affected you. My first impression of you at your brothers' weddings was when I overheard you speaking to the staff in Italian. I glimpsed Gigia that day. You've given me your heart and your body, but I'm greedy. I want it all. When you agree to marry me tomorrow, I don't want just Gigi. I want that strong, passionate Venetian I know is inside you."

Gigi went up on her tiptoes and rained kisses on his face while saying something passionately in Italian. Kane didn't understand a word of it, but it didn't require translation.

Kane's cell phone beeped with a text message. He paraphrased the message for Gigi. "Rocco said the cleaning staff has also arrived, and people are starting to get antsy. He's not sure how long he can hold them off. He suggested we either come out and greet everyone or sneak out the back door. I'll do whatever you're comfortable with."

Gigi squared her shoulders and gave him one final light

kiss on the lips. "I don't care what anyone thinks, and I'm never going to hide again. Let's go greet the family."

They linked hands and walked out the front door together. A hush fell over the large crowd that was gathered there. Someone started clapping and more and more joined in until their approval thundered over Kane and Gigi like waves crashing on a beach.

Kane spotted Gio standing off to one side with Julia. His friend nodded briefly and smiled down at his wife.

Since the moment Kane had met Gigi he'd felt as if he'd done a hundred things wrong, but suddenly it all felt right. No, theirs hadn't been the smoothest of paths, but maybe it had taken each one of those challenges to bring them to a place where nothing was impossible.

Chapter Twenty-Five

THAT EVENING AND the next morning, Gigi and Kane were given remarkably little time together. Gigi was swept off to Gio and Julia's Slater Island home. Gio invited Kane to stay at Nick and Rena's. All five of the homes buzzed with staff who were preparing for a party that would rival any wedding, even the quadruple one that had occurred there nearly four years earlier.

Gigi had breakfast with her brothers and their wives. At first she felt badly that Kane hadn't been invited, but it gave her a chance to talk about the house they'd given her. At first they weren't thrilled that Kane had preempted their surprise, but when they saw how happy Gigi was, they couldn't stop singing his praises.

She wanted to tell them they didn't have to sell him to her, but she held her tongue. It was sweet to hear even Gio list Kane's good qualities as if Gigi were still undecided.

Around noon, Leora arrived. Gigi greeted her in Italian for the first time in almost fifteen years and her mother burst into grateful tears and began thanking saints profusely.

"Mamma," Gigi said softly in her native tongue, "I'm so

sorry. I know I said it before, but it needs to be said again. Maybe a thousand more times."

Leora hugged Gigi tightly. "There is nothing to be sorry for, Gigia. Nothing."

Gigi clung to her mother. "I judged you, Mamma, and I blamed you for so many things that were not your fault. How can you ever forgive me?"

"Loving you makes it easy," her mother said before releasing her and wiping the tears from her cheeks. "Enough of this. I didn't fly all this way to cry. I came for a celebration. Kane is going to propose to you today. Are you ready for this next step in your life?"

"More than I can express in words. I woke up this morning terrified I'd discover it was all a dream. Can life be this good?"

Her mother touched one of her cheeks gently. "At times, yes. You'll face challenges, Gigia. Even with a strong man at your side. Life is not always easy. Nor is love. But relish every moment of both. The memories you make now will carry you through whatever comes later."

"You really loved Papa, didn't you?"

"Yes. I really did. And he loved us."

In the past, that claim had been an impossible one for Gigi to agree with, but this time she accepted it. Her own experience with love had shown her that in some ways it was more complicated than she'd ever imagined and in others simplistically beautiful at the same time.

It arrived without invitation.

Made no apology for its existence.

And could be a person's greatest weakness or their greatest strength, depending on whether one embraced or denied it. She met her mother's eyes and said, "I understand now, Mamma. I would love Kane even without a promise of marriage. In every way that matters, I've already said yes to our future together."

Her mother frowned. "Don't let my choices be yours, Gigia. You deserve more than I had with your father. Your children deserve a father they can be proud of. Kane is a good man. He can give you all of that."

Love—so complex and yet so simple. Her mother wanted better for her than she'd had for herself. That realization was humbling. "Don't worry, Mamma. I doubt Kane will let me leave today without agreeing to marry him."

Elise and Katrine walked over to greet Leora. They must have overheard Gigi's last statement, because Elise said, "It's the sauce. I told you it would work."

Gigi introduced her mother to her two aunts before saying, "I don't know if the sauce can be credited for this one."

Katrine waved a finger at Gigi. "You did give it to him, didn't you? Just as we suggested?"

Gigi thought back to the night she'd thrown the container of sauce at Kane. "I gave it to him, but . . ."

Elise laughed and winked at Leora. "Oo la la, you raised a wild one."

"You have no idea," Gigi said mischievously, and the older women shared a quick look of surprise.

Katrine turned to Leora. "I know that expression. Elise, this one may not need our talk."

IN THE LIBRARY of Nick's home, Kane patted his suit jacket pocket to make sure he still had the ring box. He wasn't a nervous man by nature, but his hands were cold and shaky. He hadn't been alone with Gigi since the day before, and that had given him time to consider the possibility that he should have proposed before the family descended on them.

Gigi was prone to bolting. What if they somehow sent her over the edge?

His father came to stand beside him. "Are you going to make it?"

Kane patted the pocket of his jacket once more. "Maybe."

His father gave him a pat on the shoulder. "It'll all work out. I was a wreck when I asked your mother. Want one final piece of advice?"

Kane nodded.

"There are a lot of people here with a lot of expectations. They don't matter. You do this the way you want to."

Kane hugged his father briefly. He hoped he would be even half the parent his father had been. "Thanks, Dad."

A few minutes later, Kane met Gigi in the hallway. He knew everyone was gathering on the lawn outside of Nick's house in anticipation of witnessing the proposal.

Kane held out his hand to Gigi. She placed hers in his and smiled up at him. She looked as nervous as he felt.

Following his father's advice, he pulled her into the coat closet, flipped on the light, and closed the door behind him. Gigi's eyes were dancing with laughter and his nervousness fell away. He dropped onto one knee and presented the open ring box to her. "Gigia Bassano, I love you more than I will ever be able to fully express. Say you'll marry me."

Gigi's hand trembled in his. "I will. Not only because I can't imagine spending another day without you, but also because I am more me with you than I have ever been me with me." She stopped and frowned. "Does that make sense?"

Kane took the diamond ring and slid it on Gigi's finger. He rose to his feet. "I'm more me with you than I was with me, too." Then he kissed her soundly.

There was a tentative knock on the door. From the other side of it, Julia called out. "I don't want to rush you two, but Gio sent me in here to find you, and I'd rather not tell him you're hiding in the hall closet. I'm not coming in this time, but you might want to come out before people start looking for you."

Gigi started laughing and Kane joined in.

Their love didn't need to make sense to anyone else, it made sense to them.

✧ ✧ ✧

HAND IN HAND they stepped out of the coat closet. Gigi held her left hand up to show Julia her engagement ring and received a crushing hug from her.

A moment later Kane was the recipient of the exact same embrace. Gio walked up behind Julia. Gigi showed him her ring and threw her arms around his waist, hugging him as warmly as Julia had her. Above her head, Gio met Kane's eyes and smiled. It wasn't his usual restrained expression. His eyes were shining with love for his sister, his wife, and—Kane knew—his best friend. Kane was touched by the sight of his friend finally truly happy.

Before he made an ass of himself and started getting all emotional too, Kane cleared his thoughts and said, "I hear everyone is waiting for us outside. Let's go make our announcement, Gigi."

Gigi turned with a teary smile and took his hand again. "Absolutely." Then she stopped and asked Julia, "Have you seen Annelise?"

With a twinkle in her eye, Julia said, "I saw her outside a few minutes ago. She and Waffle seem to be getting along quite well."

"Waffle?" Kane asked, not sure he liked the idea of Annelise with anyone named after a breakfast food. "The cab driver?"

Gio put his arm around Julia. "He's not so bad, Kane. Once you get to know him, he's actually brilliant in his own way. Max has been tossing the idea around of partnering with him on a pastry business. I'm not sure how profitable it will be, but the kid is convinced it would make the world a better place."

After a brief laugh, all four of them headed out onto the terrace. Family and friends were gathered on the front lawn. "Look at how many people are here because they love you," Kane said to Gigi softly.

With her heart in her eyes, she looked up at him from beneath her beautifully long lashes. "I wouldn't be here if you hadn't come to Venice to get me. I don't even want to think about how close I came to missing out on all of this."

Kane raised one of her hands to his lips and kissed it. "You would have gotten here, and we would have ended up together even if you had said no that time. When something is meant to be, life has a way of circling around until we get it right."

She went up on her tiptoes and gave him a quick kiss. "You really believe that?"

He looped an arm around her shoulder and turned them both toward the crowd that was now hushed in anticipation for their announcement. "I do now."

Epilogue

A MONTH LATER Gigi was seated at a long rectangular table in the kitchen of Uncle Alessandro's house with several generations of women. She wasn't sure why they were gathered there, but her senses were in heavenly overload from the aromas of Italian dishes being whipped together by Maddy's very French husband. The irony of it was not lost on Gigi, nor was the beauty of it. The Andrades held to many traditional values, but they easily discarded the ones they considered outdated.

When Gigi had been ordered, rather than asked, to attend one Andrade dinner a month, she'd balked at first. She and Kane had decided to split their time between Scotland and the States, but she didn't like being told what to do.

That feeling instantly dissolved as soon as she and Kane had arrived that morning and were greeted as if they had been away for months rather than weeks. Yes, this side of her family took some getting used to, but they loved her openly and in a way that left no room for doubt in her heart. Gigi needed that kind of reassurance, and they seemed to not only understand that, but also accept it about her.

❖ ❖ ❖

Her cousin Maddy stood and clapped her hands. "Who are we waiting for?"

A simply dressed, beautiful brunette bounced a young girl on her lap and said, "Lil and Jake are running late."

Maddy looked across at Gigi. "You've met Abby Corisi, haven't you, Gigi? She and her sister, Lil, are honorary Andrades."

Abby winked at Gigi. "As if this family needs more."

Gigi smiled and nodded. She vaguely remembered being introduced to the woman before. Her head still spun with the names of all the people she'd met over the last few months. "It's nice to see you again, Abby."

Rena glanced at the door. "Is Alethea coming?"

"Alethea?" Gigi asked.

Julia leaned toward Gigi and explained, "She's a good friend, also. You'd know if you'd met her. She's a tall redhead. Beautiful, but a little intense. She works for Abby and her husband."

Abby picked a carrot stick off the plate in front of her. "Yes, she's part of our security team. She and Marc are actually out with Judy today. There's nothing my daughter likes better than pretending to be a spy."

A memory came flooding back to Gigi. "I think I met her once at the weddings on Slater Island. A woman came up to me and gave me her card. She told me she knew who I was, wouldn't out me, but was there if I needed her."

Rena chuckled. "That sounds like Alethea."

Maddy clapped again. "Okay, so, do we at least have one

person from every team represented?"

Gigi searched the faces of the women at the table. "You have teams? For what?"

Her cousin Nicole laid her hand on Gigi's and gave it a sympathetic squeeze. "Oh, sweetie, welcome to the really crazy side of your family."

Tara sat back in her chair and rolled her eyes. "You say that as if your team isn't totally into this. Didn't you send Greg Banner over to Scotland about a hundred times? Not very subtle."

Julia folded her hands on the table and grinned. "That's probably why we won."

Gigi cocked her head to one side in confusion. "Greg Banner? The man who kept bringing us items to sell off one at a time? You sent him? Why?"

"We hoped you'd fall for him," Maddy said as if it were a perfectly normal thing to do.

Abby turned to Julia. "What do you mean you won?"

Julia wiggled her eyebrows up and down. "I sent Kane to get Gigi. If I hadn't, they wouldn't be together. Which means Nicole, Maddy, and I get the point. Ergo, we are officially the best family matchmakers."

Gigi raised both hands in the air. She didn't like the sound of that. "Wait. You sent Kane to get me as part of some game?"

Julia laid her hand on her rounded stomach. "No, Gigi. All I was thinking about was how to get you to come back to meet us." Then she looked around and declared, "But that doesn't mean we didn't win."

"What do you win?" Gigi asked, shaking her head.

Maddy shrugged. "Just the title as best matchmaker."

Gigi rubbed her temples with both hands. "I don't really understand."

Nicole suggested, "Should we start at the beginning?"

Abby turned to Nicole. "If we do, you should tell the story. After all, it all started with you, didn't it?"

"Me?" Nicole asked with a shy smile.

"Sure," Abby said. "Loving you brought Stephan back to his family."

Nicole blushed happily. "I'd like to believe that."

Maddy hugged Nicole. "And now you're a master matchmaker, just like me."

Rena groaned with amusement. "Gigi, this family is absolutely nuts, but they mean well."

Gigi didn't disagree. She was beginning to see how much control she had over her own happiness. Interpretation was eighty percent of reality. She could look for a hidden agenda with these women. She could worry about all the things she didn't know about them, or she could choose to believe they loved her and filter their actions through that certainty.

One path led to the anxiety she'd known most of her life.

The other brought her to the place she'd always yearned to be.

Like Kane's proposal, Gigi knew her answer immediately.

I'm not going back. From now on, at every crossroads, I'll choose love.

Gigi smacked her hand down on the table. "I want to

hear about these teams, but the most important question is—which one will I be on?"

Abby leaned in with a smile and joked, "I claim Gigi, but don't we have a clear winner? And more importantly, is there anyone left to marry off?"

Maddy rubbed her chin thoughtfully as if the questions had been serious. "Are you kidding? I just won the title as the family's best matchmaker. We can't stop now. How about the Barringtons?"

Tara asked, "Who are they?"

Rena waved a finger in the air. "You're not talking about Patrice's sister's children, are you?"

Maddy nodded eagerly. "That's exactly who I'm referring to. Technically they're not related to me, but they're cousins of my cousins so to an Andrade that's family." Maddy turned to Gigi. "The Barringtons live in New England. They don't come around much, although I think Luke has kept in touch with a couple of them. The youngest one, Kyle, was at your welcome home party, Gigi. Oh my God, the more I think about this, the more it feels right."

Nicole walked over and hugged Maddy. "I want to say no, but your track record cannot be denied. I'm in."

"Me, too," each of the other women said one by one.

Me, too, Gigi thought, and happy tears filled her eyes.

I'm not on the outside anymore.

I'm in.

I am family.

THE END

Be the first to hear about my releases

ruthcardello.com/signup

One random newsletter subscriber will be chosen every month in 2015. The chosen subscriber will receive a $100 eGift Card! Sign up today by clicking on the link above!

Other Books by Ruth Cardello

The Legacy Collection:
Also available in audiobook format

Book 1: Maid for the Billionaire (available at all major eBook stores for FREE!)
Book 2: For Love or Legacy
Book 3: Bedding the Billionaire
Book 4: Saving the Sheikh
Book 5: Rise of the Billionaire
Book 6: Breaching the Billionaire: Alethea's Redemption
Recipe For Love, An Andrade Christmas Novella

Lone Star Burn Series:

Book 1: Taken, Not Spurred
Book 2: Tycoon Takedown

The Andrades:
*Also available in audiobook format

Book 1: Come Away With Me (available at all major eBook stores for FREE!)

Book 2: Home to Me

Book 3: Maximum Risk

Book 4: Somewhere Along the Way

Book 5: Loving Gigi

The Temptations:

Book 1: Twelve Days of Temptation

Book 2: Be My Temptation

Other Books:

Taken By a Trillionaire

Books by Ruth's Family Members

Did you know that my sister, Jeannette Winters, and my niece, Danielle Stewart, also write romances? Each have series that start with a FREE book. Check out them out today while waiting for my next release.

Acknowledgements

I am so grateful to everyone who was part of the process of creating *Loving Gigi*.

Thank you to:

Nicole Sanders at Trevino Creative Graphic Design for my cover. You are amazing!

My very patient beta readers. You know who you are. Thank you for kicking my butt when I need it.

My editors: Karen Lawson, Janet Hitchcock, and Marion Archer.

My Roadies for both their friendship and their feedback.

Kathleen Dubois being a promotion wonder!

My husband, Tony. Couldn't do this without you.

My children for laughing with me instead of getting upset when I burn dinner while answering emails.

My niece, Danielle Stewart, and my sister, Jeannette Winters, for joining me in self-publishing and brainstorming with me along the way. *Always better together.*

Printed in Great Britain
by Amazon